NAMESAKE

NAMESAKE

SUE MACLEOD

pajamapress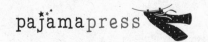

First published in the United States in 2013
Text copyright © 2013 Sue MacLeod
This edition copyright © 2013 Pajama Press Inc.
This is a first edition.
10 9 8 7 6 5 4 3 2 1

www.pajamapress.ca   info@pajamapress.ca

The publisher gratefully acknowledges the support of the Canada Council for the Arts and the Ontario Arts
Council for its publishing program. We acknowledge the financial support of the Government of Canada
through the Book Publishing Industry Development Program (BPIDP) for our publishing activities.

 Canada Council **Conseil des Arts**
for the Arts **du Canada**    **ONTARIO ARTS COUNCIL**
CONSEIL DES ARTS DE L'ONTARIO

Library and Archives Canada Cataloguing in Publication

MacLeod, Sue,
     Namesake / Sue MacLeod.
ISBN 978-1-927485-29-3
     1. Grey, Jane, Lady, 1537-1554--Juvenile fiction. I. Title.
PS8575.L49N36 2013   jC813'.54   C2012-906890-X

Publisher Cataloging-in-Publication Data (U.S.)

MacLeod, Sue,
     Namesake / Sue MacLeod.
[264] p. : cm.
Summary: Working on a history project about her namesake, Lady Jane Grey, Jane finds herself drawn to the
Tower of London and to 1553, especially whenever the present becomes unbearable.
ISBN-13: 978-1-927485-29-3
1. Self-esteem – Juvenile fiction. 2. Grey, Jane, Lady, 1537-1554 – Juvenile fiction. 3. Fantasy fiction.
I. Title.
[Fic] dc23   PZ7.M335Na 2013

Cover design–Rebecca Buchanan
Page design and formatting–Rebecca Buchanan and Martin Gould
Photo of feather–Tiina & Geir/cultura/Corbis
Cover photos–Tower of London © Marek Stefunko/Shutterstock; storm clouds © Pictureguy/Shutterstock;
vintage paper © javarman/Shutterstock; red splatter © Steve Collender/Shutterstock; wax seal © Andrey
Kuzmin/Shutterstock
Printed in Canada

Pajama Press Inc.
469 Richmond St E, Toronto Ontario, Canada
www.pajamapress.ca

For JG; and for AZ, in friendship

Prologue

She's living in one of the houses we looked at from the hill. That's where I see her in a dream sometimes—with a laptop, a phone, all the usual stuff.

In another dream I see her at a part-time job. A coffee shop downtown. She's pouring something for a customer when she glances up and sees her boyfriend in the crowd. That's why this dream's the best. I never met her "fair-haired boy," but I get to see this new guy. I like his shy smile. So does she, it seems—she pours a little too much coffee, then laughs as she wipes up the spill.

Does she slip up now and then and say a "wherefore" or a "verily"? Or does she always pull it off, this girl with pale skin and freckles? She brushes back a strand of hair. Cut short now. Dyed magenta.

What would he think, this boy from now, if he knew what I know? What would he say if he knew her last crush was an earl—an earl who wore doublets and hose instead of jeans and a jacket? And that her parents didn't really die in a car accident in England.

That's just the story we would have used.

1   Hitherto (*adverb*: up to now, to this point)

I remember what was playing in my head the day the whole thing started: nothing from the Top Nine at Nine, not like usual, but the rhyme Mr. Gregor had written on the blackboard:

> *Henry the Eighth six times was wedded.*
> *One died. One survived.*
> *Two divorced. Two beheaded.*

"Did you hear me?" Megan nudged me with her elbow. "I said, do you want to sit with those guys?"

I followed her eye to the far reaches of the Second Cup—and groaned. There was Simon Wong, who's been part of the general scenery of life ever since kindergarten, but I only knew the rest of them from history class.

"They're cool."

"That's easy for you to say, Megan. They're in all your classes."

She stuck her lower lip out. "You should be too."

Between her sulking and my mother's what-have-you-done-to-me-now look, I was sick of being reminded that I'd only gotten into Advanced Placement for one subject. Meg slipped her two biographies of Anne Boleyn into the fringed bag on her shoulder. "You should've cheated on your math exam."

"Yeah, right," I said. "You and my mom oughta join the same club."

"I don't think so." And it wasn't her words so much as the speed, or maybe the force behind them, that hung there in the air. Our eyes locked. I looked away.

Megan dug for a toonie in the pocket of her skirt, and I slung my backpack to the floor and wriggled my finger into the change compartment. I'd stuffed so many books in, you could see their shapes through the dark green material.

"Let's take this little table here," she said as I stood back up, but Simon Wong had spotted us. He was waving his arms like windshield wipers—*this* way, *this* way. By the time we got our drinks and headed over, a tall, lean guy with wavy hair was beaming at Megan. Tom something, I was pretty sure. He lifted a backpack off the chair beside him.

"Off with yer *'ead*!" he ordered when Meg slid into place. She dipped to one side with a musical sigh. When had she learned how to do that?

"And yer 'ead too!" He came lunging across the table.

"Piss off," Simon told him. "All this Tudor stuff is going to your—"

"To me what?"—groping around at the base of his neck—"Do I still 'ave one?"

"Apparently so, Tom," Meg said sweetly. "But there seems to be a shortage of brains inside."

"Aw, you sure know how to hurt a—"

"*Megan*, guess what?" A girl with a nose ring and a seriously weird name I couldn't think of butted in, with both hands cupped around her mouth. Meg hunched forward to meet her, and the Tom guy looked over their heads at me. "Have I seen you around?"

"Well, I'm in your *class*." Was I invisible? "I mean, just for History."

"Guess what, Kantor?" Simon said. "Her name's Jane Grey."

"Get out." His eyes were dark, intense. "Like that girl Gregor was talking about? Queen for a week and then they cut her head off?"

"Nine days," I said.

"Whatever. Cool. You gonna do her for your project?"

"I am." I took a sip of my Italian soda. "We're just coming from the library."

"We're just going there. I'm doing Thomas More, meself. He wrote a book called *Utopia*. And he died for what he believed in." He shrugged then, like he was trying to shrug off the seriousness that had just slipped out. Kantor, Simon had said. Tom Kantor. Had Megan told me anything about him?

He nodded at the lumpy beast perched on the chair beside me. "*Whoa*. How many have you got in there?"

And they all turned to look.

"Is it alive?" shrieked one of the blondes at the end of the table. And nose-ring girl—could it possibly be *Fluffo*? Or *Velveeta*?—hooked her grubby fingers through my backpack tab, tried to pick it up, and swooned. "It feels like boulders." Her voice was raspy and seemed to carry through the coffee shop.

"Come on, you guys." Meg's green eyes scanned the table. "Don't embarrass my friend."

Tom draped an arm around her. "No friend of yours could be an embarrassment." Which got another round of laughs. "I didn't mean she *was*," he said, but I could feel them sizing me up on that. Two weeks into high school. Jury still out.

I stared into my soda for a second to avoid their faces. I'd be glad to get myself—and my pack of boulders—home.

I caught the #7 bus to the Hydrostone and turned onto my street, Stairs Place. Needham Hill rises up at one end, a dividing line from the newer streets that spill down to the harbor. The Hydrostone is different from any other part of Halifax— twelve or so streets of row houses that are actually made of cement blocks (called hydrostone), but they look like stone, and some are painted pastel colors. Kind of Old-English-village, if you ignore the ones with vinyl siding.

My next-door neighbor was peeking through her curtain, per usual. Meg and I called her Mrs. Rachel Lynde back when we read *Anne of Green Gables*, in grade three or something. The name fit her so well, it was still how I privately thought of her. At my door, I slid my key into the lock.

Upstairs, I eased the heavy backpack off and watched it settle on my bed—hunter green against the silky blue of my new comforter.

My mother was teaching a class and she'd left me just one chore to do. "Sweetheart"—I'd checked her note on the fridge door—"need celery, dish detergent." *Sweetheart*, I thought to myself. Single Mother as Hero—Mode One.

I may as well tell you right now about the three kinds of days at our house: three whole versions of reality. There were days like this, when my mom got all affectionate and told me things about her life, and I'd tell her things—which I'd later regret saying—about mine. This was when she played the lovely widow. Single Mother as Hero. I really believe that's how she saw it.

Then there was Mode Two, the Nothing mode. Fine by me. We just didn't pay much attention to each other.

But a day could shift modes in a breath, in a heartbeat. Especially if she'd been to the Atlantica or some other hotel bar (as in, a bar her students wouldn't go to). A day could turn bad if the celery at the store was limp and stringy. Or her daughter didn't make the cut for most of the AP classes. Or tracked in some mud and didn't notice. You name it. Mode Three left a rawness behind it. A Day When Hell Broke Loose.

For now there was no Hell, at least none I knew of, lurking around the corner.

There was just me, cross-legged on the comforter I loved. I'd bought it with my money from babysitting the Hasler twins that summer. A crow cawed raucously outside my window. Another answered from across the lane, and then the chirping of some smaller birds cut in: confetti, tossed way up above the crowd.

I unzipped my pack and tipped everything out. Then I sat there for a bit, inhaling the old-paper smell of the books, and the store-fresh smell that was still off-gassing from my pencil case. I fanned the books out around me like cards. Queen of Spades, Queen of Hearts, off with 'er 'ead.

An Eyewitness guide to castles. *The Early Tudors and What They Gave Us*. *The Nine Days Queen*. A dense and dusty-looking book about the Church of England. A historical novel called *Lady Jane Grey: A 16ᵗʰ-Century Tragedy*. I flipped that one open:

> ... Jane had always liked her older cousin, Mary, whom many people shunned for holding onto the Old Faith. But now Jane didn't know what to do. The dress that Mary's messengers had brought her was exquisite: tinsel cloth of gold and velvet. It would make her brown eyes sparkle. She looked at it, draped across her bedding, and ran her hand along the folds of the skirts. Part of her wanted it, but a bigger part turned away.
>
> Jane had been raised in the New Faith; she had been taught that so bold a display of luxury was sinful. But how to refuse this gift without offending her isolated and lonely Papist cousin—

Another book seemed to be vying for my attention, its dark red cover peeking out from between two others. I pulled it out. Tiny. *Really* tiny. But thick. The scrolly letters of the title took a minute to decipher: *Booke of Prayre*.

I ran my finger over the buttery soft cover—the loops of the *o*'s, the hook of the *y*. I brought it up to my nose and breathed it in. Real leather.

Even open, it fit in the palm of my hand.

I turned a page and saw a letter *C* framed in a deep blue square, dotted with little starburst shapes. I turned a few more and saw a golden *O* framed in a square that was the prettiest shade of dusty rose, with branches growing out of it. The paper was soft. More like cotton. My throat was dry.

I'd never seen anything like this in a library—or *anyplace*.
One thing I knew for sure: I didn't take this from the shelf.

I turned it over in my hand. No stamp. No barcode. That
little slip they give you? It was coiled on the bed beside me.
No mention of any prayre booke. Twelve titles listed, and I
had—I counted them—thirteen.

"Where did you come from?"

I turned more pages and saw more blocks of color framing
some of the capital letters. Indigo, and a lighter blue. A soft
orangey red. There were *W*'s with bands of red, like bracelets.
T's with squiggly lines that made me think of branches. At
first I couldn't follow the thick, ornate shapes of the other
letters—not well enough to read anything. But I picked out
enough words to see that the *s*'s, for one thing, had long curly
tails; they looked exactly like the *f*'s. *I'll read out loud,* I figured.
That might make it easier. Like last year's English teacher made
us do for poetry, to bring the words to life:

Have mercy upon me O God
according to thy loving-kindness:
according unto the multitude of thy
tender mercies.

My eyes, they were feeling weird.

Blot out my transgressions.

They felt so heavy.

Wash me thoroughly from mine iniquity

My whole head was heavy. I had to lean back...

and cleanse me from my sin

on my pillow.

for I acknowledge my transgressions:

It was very soft.

and my sin is ever before me...

The first thing I couldn't figure out was the light.

2   Thither (*adverb*: there, to that place)

The light was flickering like a strobe, or…light on water. Was I…underwater? No, I was breathing. I breathed in. The world was green.

I fumbled around for the book. It was gone.

And my comforter. Gone. Turned into something shaggy… *grass*? A mess of roots pushed through, digging into my hip. I shifted around. Reached back for my pillow—and hit something scaly and dry. Bits of bark flaked off, like old wallpaper losing its glue.

I smacked my hands to get the grit off.

They were my hands, still. A little fuzzy at the edges.

There was a rustling. I looked up: leaves.

Leaves spinning. Slowly. Into focus.

Like the leaves around some of those letters. Dabs of light sparkling in between.

The light fell on my arms. A breeze. Warm and inviting. I sat up now and looked straight ahead. And blinked. Leaned back against the tree, and blinked again a few times. A patch of lawn rolled out in front of me. To a castle. Or a tower. Huge. Square. Ramparts on the top. Red banners flapping.

The ground—it wasn't spinning now. The world was steady. Holding steady. Bright.

The castle was studded with pebbles. They gleamed in the sun. Thick white trim, like icing, made an outline around each of its arch-shaped doors and narrow windows.

Breathe, I told myself. *Keep breathing.*

There were other buildings, to the side. Old too, but way more ordinary. Hollis Street? The government buildings down on Hollis Street—*that's* where I was. Except...the high wall, crowned with ramparts, made a border around everything. Leading back to the castle. Throwing shadows on the ground. Up-down shadows. Jack-o'-lantern teeth, they made me think of. It wouldn't be easy to get into this place.

Or out.

There was no one in sight. Just a bird, strutting on long black legs. Like a crow from my back lane. But bigger—several sizes. His beak looked sharp as a razor, and he cocked his head in my direction. "*Toc! Corronk!*"

It almost seemed like he might speak English. Tell me where I was. But he just looked around, nodding as if he owned the place. Then he zeroed in on me again, tucked back his wings, and puffed his chest out. "*Toc-toc-toc!*"

I made myself get up. Legs shaky.

Walk. A little less shaky...*keep walking.*

I made a wide circle around the bird, but his eyes were like a cold breath on the back of my neck. "*Corronk!*"

At the castle steps I stopped. Would there be people?

Would they tell me where I was and what was happening?

The door was made of planks—an arch shape that tapered to a point at the top. It loomed. Glossy black, with studs like on a dog collar.

I backed away a step. What would they think of me being

here? What if they locked me up or something?

I backed away more when the latch started to move and then the door swung open. A woman stepped out. She was stocky, wearing a brown dress that came to her ankles. A starched white scarf covered her hair. She was looking back over her shoulder. I caught a glimpse of a whitewashed wall and a tapestry—rich blues and golds like in the prayer book— before someone else appeared: a girl about my age, or maybe a few years older. The door heaved shut behind them.

The girl had a long square jaw and bushy brows above eyes that were looking right at me. Or—*seemed* to be. I couldn't see a flicker of recognition.

I swallowed.

I took a deep breath and waved my hand at her.

Still nothing.

The woman seemed to look right through me too. Then she slid her pale eyes to the girl and turned her mouth down. "Have you done now with your prattling, so we can make haste to our lady?"

Our lady?

"I crave your pardon, Mistress Ellen," said the girl.

"Hello?" My voice came out in a croak. "Hello?" I tried again. "Could you please tell me…"

They walked past me like I was made of air.

They headed across the grass and I went with them, so close they should have heard my footsteps. I could see a downy line of hair on the girl's upper lip, and broken veins on Mistress Ellen's cheeks.

We turned a corner and a row of houses came in sight. They looked cozy— whitewashed, with pitched black roofs, huddled together in an L-shape—but that's when the girl's eyes welled up. "I never believed the day would come…"

She fumbled at her waistband, yanked out a scrap of cloth, and blew her nose in it.

"Mistress Tilney"—with an impatient *tsk*—"put your muckinder away and keep your wits about you. Our lady needs our strength, not weeping."

The girl gave a final sniff and tucked the cloth away. Her clothes were finer than the woman's—creamy lace at her cuffs and slits cut in her long black skirts to show panels of blue fabric. But it was clear who called the shots between them. They bustled on. Me too.

Mistress Ellen jerked her head toward a tower that stood at the far end of the houses. This one was round. Much smaller and less fancy than the other. She seemed to be looking at a ring of windows crouched beneath its roof. "His tears alone would fill a moat, they say. The sniveling young milksop."

"I think it *sweet* that he be weeping for our lady."

"Are you daft? More for the crown that he shan't wear. The boy who would be king. Indeed!"

Mistress Tilney's brows shot up. She smirked. "It doth appear that I have knowledge you aren't privy to."

"The gossiping of ladies' maids, I daresay."

"As true as blood upon the sheets." She stuck her chin out, and they carried on in silence. Now and then she stole a glance at Mistress Ellen, whose mouth was set in a frown.

It gradually changed to a begrudging smile. "Out with it."

"Nay. It be naught but gossip."

"Very well."

A few more steps and Mistress Tilney couldn't help herself.

She glanced around the empty courtyard. "They say he sitteth in his poor, mean cell, scratching one word in the wall. The same word o'er and o'er—our lady's name."

"What *is* it? What's your lady's name?" I burst out. But of course—no answer.

Mistress Ellen sucked air through her teeth, still looking unconvinced. But softer. She squinted at the ring of windows. "When the Good Lord meted parents out, that poor lad fared no better than our own dear lady."

We were nearing the houses, with their exposed beams and pretty diamond-paned windows. But the light must have shifted. What stood out most of all now was the stone wall rising up behind them. More ramparts, on top.

How *was* I getting home from here?

We passed another wall, waist-high, with roses clinging to the side. White roses. Thick with perfume. The smell was so real—more real than *I* was here. And the colors so sharp. I hung back for a second, just taking it all in. Even the feather that was gleaming in the grass nearby—that bird's, from earlier?—long and so black that it was nearly purple. I knelt to scoop it up. When I got home—when I *did* get home—it would be great for Sara Hasler's collection.

And that's who I thought she was at first. She was so small, I thought she was one of the twins I babysat. What was *she* doing here, coming out of one of those houses? And where did she get that amazing black outfit?

But as the girl got closer I could see she was petite, but not a ten-year-old. She was more like my age. Big brown eyes, a bit protruding. A pale, freckled face.

"Who goes there?" she asked, and they both looked around.

"Where do you mean, my lady?"

I looked around too. There was no one. Just me, standing up now, sticking the feather in my pocket.

"Right behind you, pray tell."

"There be nobody here but our own two selves," said Mistress Tilney with a squeal of laughter, and Mistress Ellen bustled over, making cooing sounds. She pressed one plump hand against the girl's forehead. "Have you been feverish again? Fear not. All this madness would lead anyone to be seeing apparitions."

The eyes below the velvet headdress blinked with hurt. "I do *not* see apparitions."

She brushed her way past the two of them and stood with one white-gloved hand on each hip, taking in every detail of me from my straight, chin-length hair all the way to my sock feet. I was wearing jeans and a white peasant top—a vintage thing with gauzy sleeves that was actually more Megan's style. Actually, it *was* Megan's. I looked away from the girl's unblinking stare to their two blank faces hovering in the background, then down to the odd duck-bill toes of her boots, planted on the grass between us.

She stared at my legs. "Are you a lad?"

Her intense brown eyes moved up again. "Are you a maid like me?"

"I, uh..." I couldn't seem to get a word out. I threw my hands up and—

"Mercy!" Her hand flew to her throat. "Are you an angel?"

There was a ringing noise. Again. Again. She didn't seem to notice. I looked around to see where it was coming from...

and...

I was lying down. I didn't remember falling. Did I…fall?
The grass beneath me felt like…silk. Was…blue. I fumbled.
For…my *phone*. On the bed beside me. That's what was—what
had been—ringing.

I checked. Meg. I had a foggy thought about calling her
back, except…

across the room…

a red light. Turning into numbers: eight and four and nine.
My clock. That slammed me fully back into reality. It was 8:49.

My mom would be home soon.

I hadn't made it to the store yet.

Mode Three (All Hell) might soon be breaking loose.

I groped around and picked the little book up from the floor
where it had fallen. I started to lay it on my bed with the others,
but just held it for a second first, feeling its perfect weight in my
hand. I opened the top drawer of my night table and slipped it in.

In the bathroom, I ran a comb through my bangs. But the
teeth seemed to glide over them, not touching. I had to hurry,
but it felt like I was moving through incredibly thick air and it
made me clumsy. After I splashed my face a few times, things
started to seem crisper. *That was so vivid. That was so weird.* I
focused on the mirror, on my gray eyes and small features, and
what Megan—true friend that she is—describes as my "fine,
clear skin." Except for the cluster of zits that keeps sprouting
at the corner of my mouth.

An angel? Yeah, right.

I was heading up Young Street, nearly at the Superstore, when I
ran into Theresa with her new boyfriend.

"Hey, Theres"—I caught myself—"Traci." Her name had started morphing in grade nine, and over the summer she'd stopped answering to the old one.

"Did you hear about the tryouts?" she asked. I was still a bit fuzzy. But Dane was beaming down at her with that crooked grin of his and everything was normal. Traffic streaming by. The plain old ugliness of that corner, with its service stations and a car lot. Traci's fast-moving, glossy pink lips. The last haze of the dream blew off and I was back on solid concrete.

The light changed. We finished talking and I turned to step off the curb. A burst of laughter from Traci stopped me.

"Jane? Is that part of some new fashion statement?"

"What are you talking about?"

She unwrapped her arm from around Dane's waist and pointed. "That feather." A gust of wind came up and tossed her dark blonde ponytail. "That feather sticking out of your pocket."

3   Dissuade (*verb*: persuade, give advice)

Lady Jane Grey didn't want the throne. She was put there by her parents and their friend, the Duke of Northumberland. (They had already forced her to marry the Duke's son, Guildford.)

Jane had been at King Henry's Court since she was nine. She used to play with her cousin Edward, Henry's only son. He became king when Henry died, but he was still a boy, so he had a "protector" to advise him. Unfortunately, this was the Duke. He convinced Edward to name Jane as his successor. When Edward (who had always been "sickly") died, Jane was pronounced queen. But two of her cousins were ahead of her in line: Mary (Henry's daughter from his first wife, Catherine) and Elizabeth (from his second wife, Anne Boleyn).

Jane was fifteen—tinny, even for her time, and she had freckles (which were considered quiet unattractive). She'd been pushed into accepting the Crown, but she could be strong-willed and stubborn. In her nine days on the throne, she let Guildford be her "consort" only, not her king. She refused to give him (or his father) that much power.

Tom Kantor flipped through my draft—four pages already—and whistled. "Do you always work so hard?"

Not this again. But I glanced over at him and my heart did a skip. He was looking at me, serious and questioning, sitting on the couch beneath my mother's big Picasso print, *Three Musicians*. He was long-limbed and mysterious like they were, but softer, with his wavy hair.

This was the first of the peer-editing sessions Mr. Gregor had assigned, and I was getting my turn to host over with. My mother taught two classes back to back and I knew she'd never bail—not so early in the term.

We were supposed to bring our research materials, but I'd left one of mine—the little book—upstairs. All week, I'd been trying to fall asleep reading it. But nothing was happening. *I'm not an angel,* I needed to tell her. *I'm a girl like you.* And I needed to ask, *Can you possibly be who I* think?

Here in the normal world, Tom cracked his gum. "This peer editing's a bit of overkill. But hey, I like the pizza and everything."

Meg's voice drifted in from the kitchen. Read: "and everything."

"And my Caesar salad isn't bad either," I told him, "if I do say so."

"Sorry, kid. I don't do green."

He must have caught the look that crossed my face. "Hey, nothing personal."

I shrugged. "Doesn't matter to me if you get scurvy." I sorted busily through the papers on my lap. Would it just sit there? Loser in a Wooden Bowl. I'd made it while Meg was making the pizza dough, then escaped to the living room (and Tom) when Crisco showed up.

There was silence—growing louder. Just the *scritch-scratch* of Tom's pen. And chopping and sizzling from the kitchen.

"You're thinking of oranges."

I looked up. "Excuse me?"

"It's lack of vitamin C that gives people scurvy. Lack of fruit and stuff. Or maybe you meant to say rickets."

"Oh. Maybe. No doubt."

More silence.

I scanned his bibliography, which was very long. And *he* was onto *me* about being a keener? I put it aside and opened a folder of sketches marked Crisco Dieppe. *Wow—*

A shriek of laughter from the kitchen made me jump. It was joined by another laugh that sounded like a Canada goose with a head cold.

Tom raised an eyebrow. "What are those two up to?"

"Jane?" It was Crisco in the doorway. "Your mom's got a whole whack of beer in the fridge. Think she'd miss a couple?"

Meg was right behind her. "Yup, she'd miss 'em." She tugged her new friend back over the threshold by the purple scarf that was looped around her head.

A week ago, I barely knew who she was. Like Tom, she'd come from a different junior high than we did. Now you could hardly see Meg in the hallways of Citadel High without her. She'd been Christina till grade six, or so the story went, when she'd done some presentation on *The Count of Monte Cristo*—and kept saying it wrong. I'd add (but only to myself) that her skin was slick and shiny, stretched over prominent cheekbones. Just *like* a slab of shortening.

"Crisco," I called and she spun back into sight, twirling the cheese grater, which was studded with curls of mozzarella.

"These drawings are awesome," I told her. They *were*. I waved her sketches of Henry VIII, changing gradually from

young and handsome, if you like the burly type, to old and
bloated. She'd even done a small and gruesomely precise full-
color drawing of his grossest feature: "Enlarged Detail: The
Open Sore on His Majesty's Leg."

"Can you imagine?" She made a retching sound. "Marrying someone hot as that, and ending up with…that?"

The doorbell rang and she marched across the room like
she owned the place, grater still swinging. "Lord Simon!" She
curtsied low as she opened the door.

"Food smells great." Simon pulled off his baseball cap and
the electric red tips of his hair sprang into place. Our peer-
editing group was complete.

Crisco sashayed back to the kitchen, and Tom nodded
at Simon. "Wong," he said—that one-word way guys greet
each other. His olive green sweatshirt made his eyes an even
deeper brown.

He tucked a pen behind his ear and frowned down at
my draft, looking all professional. "You"—he aimed another
pen at me—"look like you've been counting on spell check.
Don't shoot me, please. But you've got *tinny* where you mean
tiny, and *quiet* where you mean *quite*." Then he stuck that pen
behind his other ear, and Simon and I broke out laughing.

"You"—I aimed a finger—"look ridicu—"

"*Wha*—?" He snatched both pens away without meeting
our eyes.

You had to feel for him. "At least you *looked* like an editor," I offered.

"That's my plan, you know." He leaned toward me, cheeks
slightly flushed. "I figure my timing's just right. When I finish
university and get a few years' experience, Jann Wenner'll be

ready to retire, and I'll step in as the next editor of"—a little drum roll on his knee—"*Rolling Stone.*" He grinned, like he was joking. I wasn't so sure.

"What do *you* want to do, Jane?"

"Well, I don't know, but—"

His eyes shifted. Megan, in the doorway.

"Pizza's ready." She pulled the banana clip from her hair and shook it loose. I watched him while he watched it, well, cascade.

For a minute I saw her almost like a stranger, this new-and-constantly-improving Megan. Time flipped back—seven or eight years, I mean—and I saw three kids, Megan, Theresa, and me, playing in the back lanes and on the grassy boulevards of the Hydrostone, and putting little skits on for our parents. Now Megan had reclaimed the drama that used to come so naturally. And she'd mixed it in with new stuff, like the pearly eye shadow that looked great with her creamy skin.

Crisco gave a muffled clap in my mother's oven mitts. "M'lords and ladies, dinner is served."

We were loading the dishwasher when I heard the back door open.

My stomach clenched. "Mom?"

Across the room, Megan fumbled and nearly dropped the cutting board she was wiping down.

"Did you let your class out early?" My voice came out in a squeak.

"Can you believe it?" Mom took off her jacket. "The projector wasn't working, and there was no one in AV to be found." (She had a running battle with the audio-visual

department at Mount Saint Vincent University.) She hung the
jacket on the hall tree, neatly, but not in an overly measured
way—not like trying to prove she could walk a straight line
or something. I was starting to breathe easier.

"Jane, honey." She smoothed her hair down and looked
around with a widening smile.

Mode One, full force.

I breathed easier for sure.

I could see us through her eyes: a group of straight-A
kids—well, yours truly excluded—getting together to work
on our projects. Her idea of perfect teen life.

I was scraping out the salad bowl—nearly empty, Mr.
Rickets—when she reached into the freezer and got two con-
tainers of her specialty. "Any takers for some blueberry crisp?"

Later, when people were getting ready to leave, she perched
on the arm of the couch (Mode One, holding) and listened
to Crisco yammer on about art. I zoned out then and drifted
away to a castle, a latch swinging open. A pale girl in a velvet
headdress, long full skirts...Had I *really*? Yes, I'd been there.
I had really been there.

Next thing I heard, my mom was quizzing Tom about
his whole life story, drawing him out in that way she was so
good at. A Jewish family...Brooklyn...how his parents became
Buddhist and moved to Halifax because of the big American
Buddhist community here. Did I miss anything important?

"Wow, Jane," Crisco whispered later at the door, "your
mom's a-maz-ing." From the brightness that sprang to my
mother's eyes, I knew she'd heard.

Megan looked at me; I felt it but avoided looking back.
She stepped out to the porch to wait for Simon, who was

walking home in the same direction. Tom caught a ride with Crisco when her dad came. And the house went still.

"Keep me company? While I make some dip for tomorrow night?" Mom asked.

I hesitated. I was thinking about Megan, how she tried to make me open up about stuff I just couldn't admit to—not even to her. *Why do you make things so hard for me?* part of me wanted to snap at my mother, but another part looked into her smiling hazel eyes and said, "Yeah, sure."

Thing is, there was something so beautiful about her. Not just her good looks and thick, chestnut hair, but also the rise and fall of her voice, and a kind of gracefulness to her movements.

"...So she came to my office in tears..." Our kitchen was so cozy and my second helping of blueberry crisp so tart and crunchy, I didn't even mind a story where Mom would come out looking good. And I only blanched a little when she reached into the cupboard for her scotch.

"Nightcap," she murmured. And likely nothing more would come of it. "Where was I?" she asked me. "Oh, right. So she said, 'I've looked all over for my flash drive with that paper on it, Dr. Grey, and it's disappeared into thin air.' And I told her, 'Marnie, it can't have, or so has your mark.' Did I say she hadn't printed it?" I nodded. "I told her, 'Think again, think harder. Go back to exactly what you were doing the last time you saw it.'" She waved a celery stalk. "'Face exactly where you were facing the last time—'"

The landline rang, and I glanced at the call display. "Dave?"

She nodded, and as she took the receiver—"Hello, babe"—a thought formed in my mind.

"Hey—I'll see you a bit later, Mom."

As I headed for the stairs I heard her tone shift. "What do you mean you can't make it?" But I was too distracted to give it any thought.

In my room, I settled on my patch of blue and reached into my night-table drawer for the book. The feather was lying beside it. My souvenir. My proof. Long and kind of greasy looking. I ran my thumb down the plasticky spine of it, and felt a shiver up *my* spine.

I could nearly feel the ramparts closing in.

But the book—it was way too beautiful to cause any harm. *Right?* In spite of the dryness in my throat, I opened the buttery red cover. I shut my eyes. Took a breath. Focused on what my mom had said. I sat back against my pillow. Halfway back. Like I was pretty sure I'd done the first time. And turned to what I knew was the exact same passage. Psalm 51.

> *Have mercy upon me O God*
> *according to thy loving-kindness:*
> *according unto the multitude of thy*
> *tender mercies…*

Nothing happening. I bit my lip in disappointment.

Wait. There was one more thing to try. My heart beat harder.

I started reading it out loud.

4   Truly-falsely (*adverb*: with faithful heart but incorrect speech)

I landed on my feet this time.

The world was tilting, spinning.

Breathe. Breathe deep.

A line of shadow slithered at the edge of things. It shot straight up and snaked into an up-down row. The ramparts.

A flick of red—a banner? And more banners, twitching. I spread out my arms to keep my balance. There was grass beneath me—grass, for sure, but moving. Like an ocean. I closed my eyes until the world slowed down. Or I could get myself in pace with it.

When I looked again, the waves of grass were settling, nearly still. The castle was gleaming. Huge. Proud. The turrets had stopped rippling. I heard a clanging somewhere, metal striking metal. And the whining of a hinge or wheel.

A green shape near the castle was still filling in. It rippled; it burst into *tree*. I saw someone—her, the girl, the lady—standing in the shade of it.

I hollered, "Hey!" and she turned to look at me—and froze. She could definitely still see me.

So could someone else: that bird again; its cold eye seemed to be trained in my direction. Then it hopped across the grass toward the girl—a hop and then a flurry of low flight, just a couple of feet above ground, and then a hop again. It circled her. Wings pumping to propel itself, it leapt up, nosing at—or *pecking* at?—her waist, her hands. So big beside her. "Nay. Be gone," I heard her say, and I was running. "Hey! Get out!" I swung one arm and then the other. I hit the long, stiff tail feathers.

The bird did a weird kind of spin and wheeled at me, beak open. "*Toc-toc-toc!*" A smell like raw meat hit me and I reeled back, not so brave now. But—

Phew. It dropped to the ground and then flew away—sort of—very low, touching down every couple of feet to get a kick-start.

The girl—she was on her knees.

"Are you okay?" I asked. My own heart was still pounding.

She pressed her white-gloved hands together and bowed her head.

"Oh. No," I said. "Don't pray to me."

Her forehead creased as she peered up.

"I'm not an angel. Look, get up, okay?" I offered her my hand but she said, "Nay!" and shrank away like it might burn her.

"I'm just a girl like—just a maid like you." I turned, full circle. "See? No wings."

She cocked her head and her brown eyes narrowed. "Be this a trick, then? Have you come to test me? I know my Scriptures well enough to know a messenger of God need not be wingéd."

"Oh." I didn't know what to say to that.

"What are you, pray, if not an angel?" She got to her feet, keeping her eyes on me to make sure I didn't come any closer.

"How can it be that Mistress Tilney and my nurse could see you not? They believed I had taken full leave of my senses." She looked away a second. "Mayhap they were right."

"No, no. They *weren't*. I thought this was a dream. I thought it had to be. But it's real."

Her pale cheeks were flushed with color as she looked at me, and her headdress was knocked askew a bit above her sandy hair.

I pointed to the tree where I'd landed before—it was a week ago now—and where she'd been when I arrived today. "See, I *remember* that. And *that*." I pointed to the castle, where the bird had gone now, sulking, blending in against the glossy black paint on the door. "I *am* here. I can smell the grass." I looked up. "I can feel the sun on my face." But was this proving something? "Am I not here?" I asked her. "Aren't I?"

"True as life. If"—she paused—"if mine own witness can be trusted."

Right. We stood facing each other.

A few seconds passed, and she raised an eyebrow. "Thou art real enough to have frightened Odin."

"Odin?"

"Yea." She pointed to the castle doorway. I could make out a jabbing motion, the bird pecking at itself.

"He was looking for his egg. I bring him some, by times. Or meat. He meant no harm."

I felt like some big jerk then, five-foot-five of me towering over her five-foot-nothing. "I didn't mean to scare...I'm sorry...Odin. I just meant, I guess, to save you."

"'Twould be a welcome change that anyone should try to save me." A smile flickered across her face. But what a sad smile.

Are you who I think? I had to look away, toward the castle. "Your Odin doesn't fly too well."

"Do you not know?"

"Know what?"

She flipped her hands up. "How can you be standing here in front of me and know nothing of the Tower? Wherefore do you speak so strangely? Do you know nothing of the world?"

"No," I admitted. "I don't even know what year it is."

"The year of our Lord, fifteen hundred fifty-three. Art thou the queen's new fool, then?"

It was the exact right date. "Queen...Mary?"

"Long may she live, Her Grace, my cousin. She rides here this day from Suffolk to claim her rightful crown."

"Your Grace"—I started.

"*Sshhh!*"

It was clearly the wrong thing to call her.

There was no one in sight except for two men hauling a cart, too far away to hear us. But from the wild look in her eyes you'd think the sparrows in the grass, and even the *blades* of grass, were listening. "I be no longer Queen of England. Her Grace my cousin—did I say it not?—she rides here as we speak. Wilt thou have my head laid on the block? And thine own alongside it for good measure?"

No need to wonder now if she was who I thought.

Or where we were in her story.

My mind scrolled back over what I'd read. It was a couple of weeks ago, then, that the young King Edward had died, and Lady Jane's parents woke her and took her, by barge, to the Duke of Northumberland's estate house. I could imagine waves lapping in the River Thames. No light except from

lanterns and maybe a column of moonlight. No idea where
she was being taken. The most powerful people of the Court
got on their knees when she arrived and called her queen. The
lords and ladies. She kept saying no, but they kept insisting.

She crossed her hands now at the low, square neckline of
her dress as if to calm her heartbeat. Same dress, I registered
vaguely, as last time.

And I'd read about them bringing her here—to the Tower
of London—in daylight. A flotilla of barges on the Thames
to show the people their new queen. A small queen in high
platform shoes so they could see her. But why *her*, the people
thought, instead of Mary, or Elizabeth? The cheering and
applause was faint and scattered.

She clenched her hands now, and unclenched them. Same
white gloves as last time.

The light was so clear and the walls of the castle so clean
and pearly, you'd think this was a safe place. A sane one. A
hint of perfume hung on the breeze from those white roses.
Same warm breeze on my arms, too, as before. *Could time be
standing still here?*

"When did we talk before?" I asked. "Was it…today?"

"Nay!" And what a look she gave me. "'Twas a fortnight past."

Two weeks. Time here was moving *twice* as fast? I was ready
to believe anything.

"You must be mad indeed."

I had to shrug. It could be possible.

"God willing that you *were* a fool," she said, "or a court
jester." She was taking me in again, lips pursed, considering.
"Or a mummer? Yea, could that be it? Are you from the
Christmas Revels?" Another smile was forming. Hopeful.

Small. "Are you with Blunderbore and Jack? Has someone sent you to amuse me?"

I had no clue what she was talking about. But I did know that smile—the kind that waits, halfway, until the other person meets it. Over her shoulder, a movement at the castle door—

She followed my eye, turning as a man came down the steps, Odin fluttering out of the way.

"The Marquis of Winchester." Her voice quavered. "The Lord Treasurer."

The cape around his shoulders seemed to undulate as he got closer, heading straight for us. God, he didn't *see* me? *Thine own alongside it*—her words came back to me—*for good measure.* I took a breath that felt like all the breath I had. I raised my hand and waved.

He didn't blink.

"My lord," she said as he came up to us.

"My lady."

He gave her a stiff little bow. From the sneer playing on his lips, he didn't mean much by it. He had the strangest beard, two triangles ("forked," I later heard it called), and his legs were stuffed like sausages into pale green tights. This reminded me, weirdly, of football players practicing on the Commons, and a nervous giggle hiccupped out. Her eyes widened, sliding to mine for half a second. Then she looked at him wagging his ring-studded finger.

"There appears to be a discrepancy in the royal treasures with which you were entrusted."

"There must be some mistake." The flowing side panel of her headdress blocked her profile now, but I could see her small, pert chin jut out. She squared her shoulders.

"We shall require restitution."

"With what, pray tell?"

"With any jewels or valuables in your possession."

"But hear me, my lord, I have taken nothing."

"And hear me well, my lady. Goods are missing from the coffers of the former queens."

His finger was still shaking. And the turrets, the turrets in the background were…shaking?

"It behooves me to say you have stepped low indeed"…her voice was fading …"to rob a woman who has lost all else"…I had to strain to hear her…"a woman on whose head 'twas you, my lord, who placed the crown—"

The grass was moving underneath me. It was me…

Me weaving in and out…"despite her own appeal"…her words a banner I could only catch the edge of…"that to do so was unseemly." Another voice kept cutting in…

"Wake up."

Something shadowy, leaning over me. "*Wake up!*"

My mother.

Thumb and finger digging, hard, into my collarbone. Gust of whiskey-breath in my face.

I used both hands to pry her off. "What *is* it?"

She stumbled backward and into my dresser. I heard a dangerous tinkling of the ornaments on top.

"What *is* it?" she mimicked.

In the light coming in from the hall, an afterimage of the blue sky and the castle's pearly surface floated, fading, leaving just my open door, a slice of my wall with posters, and my pathetic mother barely holding herself up.

"I'll tell you, Miss Jane, what it was *gonna* be. A dinner party. L'il ole dinner party at the home of the good Dr. Grey."

She burped. Brought a fist to her mouth. "Shit-box that it is, that is."

She giggled, like she'd made some clever rhyme or something, and I forced my lips into a smile. A real-looking smile, or it would set her off even more. I willed my heart to stop beating so loudly.

"But Dave"—she swayed, reached for the wall, and caught her balance—"could he make it to the dinner? For the Chair of the De-Part-Ment? Uppity bitch anyway."

As my eyes got more adjusted to the light—the world—I saw her face sag in self-pity. "Why, Jane, do I pick such losers?" Then she snapped her fingers, like she was remembering why she was here. "Speaking of…uppity. Uppity daughters. Who Drop Food On The Floor That Their Mother Has Scrubbed. Scrubbed for her…dinner party. CheeseCheeseCheese to the front door like Hansel and Gretel," she sing-songed. "Gretel, yeah. Get up."

Her hand came swiping as if to grab me by the hair, and I squirmed away, pressing into the slats of my headboard.

Don't cross another line. Please don't. I held my arms up, crossed. A shield. She teetered back a step.

"Get up," she said. "And clean it."

When I wrung out the mop and propped it to dry by the back window, the first light was starting to seep in. I tugged the blind down tight. I didn't want the world to see in. To see me. And see her. And I didn't want to watch the shadowy shapes out back fill up with color—the coloring in of a supposedly bright new day. I didn't want to see them gradually announce themselves as fences, cars, and bushes, and swing sets for happy little kids who didn't know what lay in store.

She was dozing at her desk. Head in her arms. A half-empty glass was propped on a stack of papers, dangerously close to her computer. I took it to the kitchen, started to rinse it out, even, but my hand stopped halfway to the tap. How stupid. Who cares?

"Jane," she croaked. "Help me up to bed?"

"Sure, Mom."

I hooked my arm through hers, trying to hold my face away so I wouldn't smell her. But she nuzzled up, hair brushing my cheek. Her lovely chestnut hair. I couldn't see her eyes, but I knew from her voice that they were red and puffy.

"Jane?" She sank onto her bed. "I'm so sorry if I wasn't nice."

"That's okay, Mom," I heard myself say. *That's okay, Mom?*

I went to my room to wait for morning.

5 School-doing (*noun*: training, instruction)

Mr. Gregor spun around with a piece of chalk in his hand. "Ms. Grey, how kind of you to grace us with your presence."

He was great. But why do teachers always use that same old line as if a) it was funny, and b) they'd made it up themselves?

"Take your seat. We've got a guest speaker coming in later from the guidance office." It didn't sound like this was *his* idea. "We need to move along."

I tried to walk quickly, but my eyes were stuck to the board. Round towers. Square towers. Ramparts. "The Tower of London" scrawled across the top.

He put a moat in, drawing choppy little waves.

"This big square building that looks like a castle is called the White Tower." He went over the lines to make them thick. "It's really more a pearly gray. But an impressive sight." He left an empty space for grass. "And here"—he drew a long narrow building—"is where the Crown Jewels were kept. Still are."

His blue-plaid arm swept back, swept forth—

"...*the coffers of the former queens...*"

—I tripped on something and fell forward. *My god, what was*—? *No.* It was just the floor of the classroom coming up to meet me. My books and pencil case went flying as my arms shot out.

"Jane?"—from the board—"are you okay?"

"I'm fine." I was crouched, my eyes fixed on the floor, scooping up my books, when two more hands joined in to help. Long, graceful fingers, but guy hands for sure. Leading up to thick-boned wrists and forearms laced with dark hair and—I felt my stomach fluttering—the shoved-up sleeves of an olive green sweatshirt. I looked up into his eyes. Tom Kantor's. They crinkled in a smile. I felt my cheeks go red and looked away.

"Pretty old move, Jane. Drop your books right in front of him."

This from Crisco when I slid into my seat near her and Megan. Crisco's whispers—well, all the kids around us laughed.

"I tripped on someone's backpack strap, okay?"

What nerve. To tell everyone that I liked a guy who liked my best friend. Emphasis on the *my*. And how did she know, anyhow? Was I that obvious? It was the first thing—well, nearly—that I couldn't talk to Meg about.

I snuck a glance to where Tom was sitting. *Phew.* He didn't seem to have heard. His chin was resting on his hand while he watched—intently, I hoped—as Mr. Gregor drew a line that was turning into an L-shape, turning, now that I watched it too, into a row of smallish houses, diagonally across from the White Tower.

Mr. Gregor tapped the first house with his chalk. "Henry built this as a gift for Anne Boleyn." He nodded at Megan and at the other three girls who were doing their projects on Anne. "While she was still in favor."

"She'd hardly need it after," someone wisecracked, and he smiled wryly.

"This one here"—tap of his chalk—"is Mr. Partridge's house. The Gentleman Jailer."

That was the house Lady Jane had come out of, the first time I'd seen her. His diagram was right. Though I guess he wouldn't know about the wall of roses.

"And right across—right here—is where a scaffold would be built." He drew a box and filled it in with rapid strokes for straw. "The execution site."

A sympathetic voice rang out—a girl called Yasmeen Mahvash. "Do you mean a prisoner could watch, while their own…?"

Yeah. And hear the nails being pounded. I'd already finished one of those biographies. Jane had no other window to look out of.

Mr. Gregor had moved on to labeling the towers. "Bloody Tower, Cradle Tower…" He was scribbling and drawing arrows. "Lanthorn Tower and Lion Tower, which was aptly named. It's just a ruin now." He took his eraser and rubbed part of it out. "But it used to house the Royal Menagerie. A zoo. They kept big cats, sometimes a lion. Often"—he winced—"on chains."

I winced too. *May I never see that.*

"And there were other creatures in captivity at the Tower. Less exotic. There still are." He drew a lopsided figure with drooping wings.

"What's that, sir? And what's it been drinking?"

"Is that the ghost of Anne Boleyn?"

"Ten marks off for you, Wong. And you too." He pointed

at Steve Ripley, a big guy at the back. "And anyone else who doesn't know a raven when they see one."

"I think I've seen one," Megan said.

I leaned across the aisle. "You did?" I whispered. "When?"

"I can't remember. Sometime lately."

Crisco's hand was waving.

"Yes?"

"Sorry, sir. But I took a nature drawing class this summer? And a raven's wing span is way bigger than that."

"Ms. Dieppe, you've hit the nail on the head."

"Does it still 'ave one?"

"*Can* it, Kantor. These ravens, they're known as the Tower ravens. Maybe they do have more majestic wings than what I've drawn here, as our artist"—a smug little smile crossed Crisco's lips—"has pointed out. But the fact is, their wings are clipped so they can't fly away."

"Why would anyone *do* that?" asked Stella Blakely, one of the blonde girls from the Second Cup.

"Thank you, Stella. The day's most intelligent question. There's a legend going back to the time of Charles II that if there aren't any ravens on the Tower grounds, the kingdom will fall. So even now they still keep them. Eight ravens." He grabbed a sheaf of papers from his desk and rifled through. "Here are the names of today's group. Thor, Branwen, Gundulf, Baldrick." He pronounced the strange names slowly. You could tell he enjoyed how they carried traces of another time. "Gwylum, Hugine, Munin, Bran. People thought the ravens' loud cawing would warn them if an attack was on the way. It probably goes back to the ruler of the Norse gods, who kept"—he scanned the room—"Who's up on their Norse mythology? Yes, Mr. Ripley?"

"Kept two wolves at his side and a raven on his shoulder. His name was Odin."

"*Very* good."

"But they're nasty." It was the other blonde.

"How do you mean, Alexa?"

"We went there when we went to England last year. And one of those birds kept pecking at my shoelace. And he tried to take an ice cream cone right out of my little brother's hand."

"Ghastly grim and ancient Raven wandering from the nightly shore—"

"You okay, sir?" Ripley asked, and Mr. Gregor's voice kept booming, "Tell me what thy lordly name is…"

Simon snapped his fingers. "Quoth the Raven, 'Nevermore.'"

"Good stuff, Wong. You know your Poe."

"Mr. Gregor?"

"Tom?"

"It didn't work though, did it? I mean, didn't the kingdom fall anyhow?"

"Let's take a look at that." He put his hands out as if to grab the question by its lapels. "We still have the queen, but—"

There was a tapping on the door. Through the little rectangle of window: the lacquered blonde hair of Ms. MacAllistair from Health and Guidance.

She came in, bringing a poster of a cool-looking black guy and a very skinny white girl, both gazing in apparent delight at a computer screen in the school's Wellness Center. She clipped it to the board, hiding the jailer's house and the White Tower. One wing of the droopy raven was sticking out.

6 Love-springs (*noun*: young shoots of love, youthful growth of love)

I was meeting Megan outside the gym that day at 3:30. She was late, so I sat on the steps and got a bit of writing for my project done.

Among the nobility, it wasn't unusual for a girl's parents to choose her husband, but Jane's had already betrothed her to a young earl, Edward Seymour. Then they broke that betrothal and beat her up—quite severely—to make her marry Guildford Dudley, the Duke of Northumberland's son. They treated her so badly, it's hard to imagine ~~no matter what you've been through~~

They wanted personal power, but the politics they used to get it were linked to the struggle between the New Faith (Protestant, which King Henry had founded, and Jane's tutors had taught her) and the Old Faith (called Papist, or Catholic, which her cousin Mary would bring back). Jane, a devout Protestant, would hate to see that happen. But she still refused the throne, initially, because it was Mary's, by rights.

Jane's parents and their friends convinced her to take it, though—partly by saying their lives were at stake. They had sent out announcements swearing their loyalty to Jane. So, if Mary became queen instead, she might kill them.

"Lady Jane, don't you ever go home?"

Here came the fluttering again. I knew Tom's voice before I even looked up.

"What time is it?"

He checked his cell. "It's 4:03."

"No way." I hesitated and looked around. This was definitely the right place. "I'm meeting Megan here. Half an hour ago. We're going to the mall."

He flicked a lock of hair from his eyes. "She must have forgot. I saw her leave with Crisco."

"Oh." I fiddled with the zipper on my backpack while I tried to recompose my face. It felt like someone had slapped me. I dropped in my notebook and pen. Tom's boots, I noticed, were Doc Martens. Brown and sort of dusted with clean dirt, if you know what I mean, like they spent a lot of time walking through the woods. I got up. I tried to shrug in a way that, when done by my formerly reliable best friend, looked *très* nonchalant.

"You heading home?"

I nodded.

"Mind if I walk along?"

Gulp. "Sure." I folded my jean jacket over my arm and fell into step beside him.

When we came to the lights on Bell Road, he said, "How are things going with the *real* Lady Jane?" The traffic in front of us turned into a streaming mass of colors.

"I…" *What are you talking about?* I didn't trust myself to speak. A good thing, as it turned out, because Tom kept talking.

"I'm having a hell of a time finding stuff about More's childhood and teens. Why's Gregor so big on that? I bet you're finding it easier for Jane Grey?"

Things came back into focus.

The traffic stopped and we crossed over.

"I'd hope so," I said, "since she only lived to be sixteen." It came out snarkier than I'd meant. "It *does* help me understand her," I added more softly. "*Imagine* her, I mean. Like how she loved her tutors, and they were Protestant, so…"

Wow, Jane, fascinating conversation. I let my voice trail off.

We were crossing the Commons, where the football team was just breaking up after practice. I watched them fall out of formation as they ran, turning back into separate individuals.

Tom was watching too.

"You covering the games for the school paper?"

"Nope. I'm mostly sticking to music stuff. But you know what else they asked me to do?" A small dog tore across the path in front of us. "An article on the Wellness Center."

"Why would you want to do that?"

"That's what *I* said."

The dog came streaking back with a Frisbee in its mouth.

"Hey, sweet." Tom reached out and grazed the shaggy rump as it flew past. "I think it's exploitation. Taking advantage of the new guy."

"You could do an exposé. 'Editors Exploit Rookie Reporter.'"

"Not bad." He snapped his fingers. "'Forced to Interview Helmet-Head MacAllistair and the Poster Couple.'"

"That girl looks anorexic to me," I said.

"Hey. That's my sister."

"*What?*"

"Oh, it's okay. She's always been a bag of bones."

"My god." We walked along in silence. Except for the hot, embarrassed roaring in my ears.

"What do you think"—I said—"of 'Commons Opens Up to Swallow Girl'?"

He laughed out loud. Then he glanced at me out of the corner of his eye. "That girl in the poster? I never met her in my life."

I swatted him with my jacket and he raised an arm to block me, his sweatshirt riding up to show a patch of bare skin.

Then his hand was on my shoulder, holding me in place. "Look out." Another dog was barreling toward us—a German shepherd bounding after a ball. A flock of pigeons wheeled up. You could hear the shepherd's drumming paws and rasping breath. Then he snatched the ball in his jaws in mid-air and tore back past us, and, like Tom's hand, he was gone.

I folded my jacket back over my arm. "How come *you're* late leaving school?" I asked, to break the silence. "Editorial meeting?"

"No. I was…well, actually, chess club."

"I *love* chess."

"You do?"

I nodded. "My mom taught me how to play when I was in grade five. If the game was still going she'd let me stay up late."

"Did you play as slowly as you could, then?"

"Not if I was winning." I smiled. "I get pretty competitive when it comes to chess." I remembered the clock on the kitchen wall, though. How sometimes the two hands pointed straight up and then kept going. And the crickety sounds of the fridge as we sat, hunched together at the table, woodstove glowing, back in what I think of as the Single Mother as Hero years.

I told him about it—not about Mode One, of course, but about the hands sliding past midnight. Whatever happened to that clock?

And then it came rushing at me. My mother shouting. Something sailing through the air.

"Lots of people think chess is for nerds," Tom was saying.

I stuck my nose up. "I don't know why."

"You," he said, "haven't seen the rest of the chess club."

We were walking up Agricola Street, passing Smith's Bakery where my mom used to buy my birthday cakes before I fell for Dairy Queen. That was so long ago—before she fell off the wagon. Before I even knew what "the wagon" was.

"Your mom seems cool," Tom said. "Being a prof, though, does she expect you to ace all your classes?"

"Yeah," I admitted. "And most of my marks aren't quite in the same league as the rest of you."

"You seem swift enough to me, kid."

I glowed with pleasure. A glow dimmed only by the "kid."

"You should see me in math, though," I told him.

"You should see *me* in French. Or hear me, more like it. I get by 'cause I ace the exams. But my accent sucks."

"*Non!*"

"May. Wee. And anyhow—marks. They're not the whole point of life. Will someone please tell that to my dad? Like, 'Time to Start Thinking about Good Universities.' He's so into it. I'd flunk something just to rebel, except"—he broke into a smile—"I'm kind of into it too. So, what's the deal with you and history? You've just always liked it?"

"Yeah, I guess. Stuff about how people lived. I remember in grade six," I said, "we had a project on the Halifax Explosion—"

"We had that too."

"And I got this book out of the library, about these kids, the day it happened."

"That book was great."

I think my mouth fell open. "You remember it too? What I liked best," I said, "was how she described what they were doing, before the two ships collided. And even what they were carrying in their satchels." I checked to make sure he was still with me, and he was, his dark eyes trained on mine. "I even liked the words. Their satchels."

"Cool," he said. "What *I* liked best was how people ran down to the waterfront, like it was some big show. The mushroom cloud and smoke—"

"Yeah, and how some of those guys from the French ship—"

"How they were shouting a warning—"

"Only nobody knew French."

"And then"—he closed his eyes—"*pffft.*"

"Right here." I waved my hand to take in the whole north end of Halifax, and the harbor just beyond our line of vision.

We were coming to the set of lights on Young Street. Same lights where Traci had pointed to the feather—I pushed that from my mind for now.

"Hey. You know what you were saying before about your project?"

"What was that?"

"Something about her tutors and the religion they taught her?"

I saw that serious look on his face, like I remembered from the Second Cup.

"I was thinking," he said. "All that stuff sounds so lame, till you compare it to your own life. My family's Buddhist, right? And we have this thing called Children's Day, where you put up an altar." The light turned green and he waited till we crossed. Then he waited a couple more beats. "You ever heard of this?"

"Yeah. One of my mom's old boyfriends was Buddhist. He moved here from the States too." I didn't add that she and her drinking buddies had a word, "Buddhagonians," for all those white Buddhists who had moved here, after their Tibetan leader. Cute, since "Haligonians" is what you call people from Halifax. But nothing was funny when Analise and her friends were swigging whiskey. Mocking.

"Anyhow, when my mom moved out"—he looked away for a second and counted on his fingers—"two thousand and, I don't know, first year of junior high, Dad said he just didn't have it in him to do the Children's Day thing. So Naomi and me, that's my sister—"

I shot him a look.

"My *real* sister, who's in grade six," he said, "and chubby. But don't tell her I said that."

When? When I get to meet her?

"Naomi and I got the stuff out of the basement and set up the altar ourselves. And it was good. It even made my dad feel better." He looked down at his woodsy boots. "You know, I never told anybody that."

We were now into the Hydrostone. Several blocks out of the way from where I happened to know he lived. In front of my house, he just kept standing there. I saw Mrs. Lynde's curtain slide open an extra inch.

He started shuffling a pebble around. Kicked it. Lined it up again and kicked it at my sneaker. I shot it back and—*ping*—it ricocheted off his toe. I heard myself giggle.

"I wonder if you…"

"Uh-huh?" I nodded my encouragement.

"I wonder if you'd show me which one's Megan's place. Just thought I'd drop by. See if she got home."

In my (thankfully) empty house, I went to my room and curled up on my comforter, glancing up at the photos beaming from my bulletin board. A wallet-sized shot of my dad the year he died. And a faded one—him at my age with his sister, Peggy. Among the newer shots was one I'd taken of Megan and Theresa/Traci, hamming it up at Clam Harbour Beach. Megan was spilling out of her yellow string bikini—kinda slutty, to tell the truth. I rolled the other way. My phone started ringing—kept ringing. I just let it. What kept coming back in putrid little waves was the sound of my own giggle. High. Happy. Absurd.

Later, I checked the display. Megan. Mom's work (good news: she'd made it in okay). And one from *Crisco*? What did she want?

Megan's voice was first: "Jane? Listen. I'm so sorry about the mall. I only thought of it this minute. Forgive me? And call me! I've got a mystery for us to solve."

Come on. Do you think it's that easy?

My mother sounding syrupy. "How's my best girl—" I skipped it. I wasn't in the mood.

"Hey, Jane. It's Crisco. Listen, I'm sorry about that stupid crack in class. Me and my big mouth. I'd really like it if you'd call or text me. I just got in from Megan's house…" She rattled on, but I'd quit listening.

What was this, The Feel Bad for Jane Club?

I hit Erase. Erase. Erase. And reached into my night table.

I didn't feel like talking. To anybody here.

7   Repast (*noun*: food and drink, meal)

This time I didn't even look until the world held still.

I'd landed on my butt, and what was settling into place beneath me was a rough-plank floor. A damp coldness seeped in through the seat of my jeans.

I blinked, and things came slowly into focus. A dim room, lit by smudgy light from one small window. The girl was sitting near it, with Mistress Ellen standing behind her doing something to her hair. Rain was pounding, hard. Like a band playing too loud, with Mistress Ellen's croaky voice bouncing along beside it:

> *"We made thee be-e our* Harvest Que-een
> *And* yet *thou wo-ouldst not* love *me..."*

I winced when she reached for the high notes, but the girl—it was hard to really think of her as "Lady Jane"—was more forgiving: part wince, part affectionate smile. My eyes had adjusted enough to make out details, and if she had turned her head a shade she would have seen me. But she looked straight ahead, into the room, and I looked with her.

A shallow bed on stubby legs. Hardly what a Lady would be used to. She would live here for several days or weeks—

that's what she thought at this point. Not for months. And she thought it would all end in a pardon.

I saw a trunk in one corner with a stack of books on top. I squinted, and my breath caught: at the very top, a tiny one covered in red.

There was a poky little fireplace grate; I rubbed my arms, wishing the fire was lit.

Mistress Ellen broke off singing. "Tilt down for me, kindly." She held a hank of her lady's hair up to the light, went through it strand by strand, and gave a chirp of satisfaction. "Not a nit to be seen. That biddy rake did its work."

A sniff. "For all the fuss and bother of my wedding, 'twas the only thing of use in it."

"I can give you no quarrel on that." Mistress Ellen split the hair into three sections and started braiding it. "Did you hear that the Duchess of Northumberland was in sore need of the biddy rake herself?"

"Or a lesson in manners!"

"Yea, to the point." She gave the braid a tug for emphasis.

"Ow!"

"I beg your leave, my lady. Can you credit it? Picking lice and squeezing them at table! Not to speak ill of your mother-in-law."

"Good heavens, nay. The wretched woman."

They laughed, and when their laughter faded there was just the rain. The nurse's movements, hand over hand, took on a hypnotizing quality. She coiled the finished braid into a knot and stuck it in place with a mean-looking hairpin. "There. Now let us find you a fresh headdress, to go sup with the Partridges."

The girl stood up, poking at the knot to test its firmness.

"A helping of small mead would hit the spot." Then she turned and—"Ah!"

She'd seen me.

"Did a mouse run crost your foot again?"

"Nay." Her eyes darted back and forth from me, still on the floor, to Mistress Ellen.

"What is it, then?" The woman looked at her and then at me—no—*through* me.

The girl ran the back of one hand across her forehead. "I feel faint." She crossed the room to her bed. "I must needs rest a while."

Mistress Ellen was right behind her.

"I wish to rest, I pray, in solitude."

"Have you been seeing—"

"I have not been *seeing* anything." She swung both feet up and lay flat on her back.

"God willing you are not with child."

Her head shot up. "I feel faint, I said. Not stomach-qualmed."

"You were hale until this minute. Shall I fetch your tray and eat here with you?"

"Nay!" Then her voice went softer. "Fetch it, if you will. And grant me, pray, a spell of time to rest."

After a bit more nagging and cajoling, Mistress Ellen trudged downstairs. The girl was on her feet in no time, coming toward me. Her face was bright, breath shallow. Fear, for sure, but I could also sense excitement.

"You have come again."

I was just getting to my feet, and she held her hands out and I took them. The small, warm hands of a girl nearly five hundred years dead.

I think we both shivered.

"Thou art flesh," she said after a second, "whatever else thou art."

I figured I should just come out with it. "I come from"—I forced myself to meet her eyes—"from the fu…" *No, that would sound* too *weird.* "From another time and place. I keep getting sent back here."

The air seemed to shift as she frowned at me, doing her best to take this in. And failing.

A little laugh came out. "Speaking nonsense, as before."

"No. *Really*—"

"If your task is to amuse me, you are doing passing well. I thank you." She cupped both hands around her face, her brown eyes wide, considering. "You *cannot* be a reveler. The Christmas Revelers cannot make themselves *invisible.* Mayhap"—she raised a brow, ironically—"the sorcerer John Dee has conjured you?"

"You don't *get* it. I don't even know these people."

"And I recall," she said, "that you knew not the year. You cannot be from…" She let her voice trail off. She paced around, and then pivoted back on her heel. "Were the Lord to send a messenger, he would surely not dispatch a simpleton. Not for a scholar such as me."

I'm actually "swift enough," I might have said, but she was too busy puzzling things out. "Unless"—she brought a finger to her chin—"Mayhap to teach me humility? My Lady Mother, and even my tutors. They all say I be lacking it."

She bowed her head as if I wasn't there, and started praying.

"Forgive me, Father, for my sin of pride. And especially for the one sin I truly *did* commit that night they thrust the crown upon me. My mother and my father, them whose blows still blossomed green and purple on my flesh that night"—she took a ragged breath—"the vulgar Duchess of Northumberland and her scheming duke. The rotten, plotting lot of them. Forgive"—she took another breath—"my misbegotten moment of pure pleasure, when they all fell to their knees before me."

I stood there staring. Was it appropriate to clap?

Footsteps sounded on the stairs.

She backed away on tiptoe.

When Mistress Ellen came in with the tray, fussing and muttering, her lady was resting peacefully. One arm, in its huge velvet bell of a sleeve, was hanging down. Her bare hand was curved like a half shell, grazing the floorboards.

She sat up as soon as we were alone again, reaching back to readjust her hairpin. Her forehead was high. I'd read somewhere that this was considered a sign of intelligence.

"I'm not a simpleton," I said. "I do know the year now: 1553. And I know that you're Lady Jane Grey."

"I am called Jane Dudley now."

"I know who you *are*, I mean. And that this is the Tower of London."

She hardly looked bowled over. "And *thy* name?"

"Jane," I said. "Jane Grey. Like yours."

"Is *that* what brings you here?"

I shrugged. "I don't think so. We don't look alike or anything."

My dark brown hair (thin, straight, and kind of shiny) was a contrast to her lighter hair; and my face (narrow, oblong) was very different from her heart-shaped one with full cheeks and small, dainty chin. She looked me up and down again, my modern clothes and all. I felt hyper-aware of my breath, of my *physicality*, right down to a paper cut on my index finger and a worn spot on the knee of my jeans. I was here all right, in the middle of her space, her century. But if it weren't for Odin's feather in my drawer at home, I still wouldn't believe it.

She closed her eyes. Then opened them.

"Still here," I said, and she shook her head as if to admit that it was true—though unexplainable.

The air seemed to crackle with a nervousness, a sudden shyness on both sides.

She looked away, at her tray on the stool where Mistress Ellen had set it.

"I crave your pardon. I…" She rolled her hands in the air as if to say she'd forgotten her manners. "Shall we break bread together?" Then she stopped with one hand on the lid. "Do you *eat* the food of mortals?"

"I…er…sure."

When the lid came off, a smell escaped. A wedge of cheese that looked like crumbling cement—that was part of it. Another smell, yeasty, wafted from a pewter mug. My mother staggered through my mind. There was a heel of bread, turned black. Or had it always been? And a mound of stringy meat. I felt my throat close up. "Hey, thank you. But you only have enough for one."

"Prithee! I beg of you."

Was I being as rude as the duchess? My finger hovered over the tray. The girl's full skirts—*Lady Jane's* full skirts—were sort of puffed out around her. She patted the bed next to her, inviting me to sit. I did; the blanket was scratchy. My finger still hadn't come in for a landing.

O-kay. I took a piece of meat and brought it to my mouth. Some kind of spice had been rubbed in, and the texture was chewy. Not bad, in fact. I took a little more. "This chicken's good."

"Titmouse."

I stopped mid-bite. "Excuse me?"

"Titmouse."

"You're saying I just ate a *mouse?*"

"A titmouse be a *bird*. You truly are a fool!"

I let the second piece go down, and stuck my chin up. "We don't eat titmice in my time and place."

"Your time and place." She smiled and gave a little wink.

"One thing we *do* do, though"—I snapped my fingers as the thought went through my head—"is play chess, same as you do. *We* could play sometime, and you'll see I'm no fool." I looked around the room. Dim light and smudgy window. But the chill was gone. I looked back into her intense eyes. "Next time?"

Her expression was doubtful. "I have not had a worthy opponent since I last saw my tutors." She pouted and took a sip of her drink. "Ale," she said, and pouted more. "I was hoping for small mead."

Her nails were bitten-down, I noticed—jagged-looking against the bruise-colored sheen of the mug. *How sure did she feel about that pardon?* There was so much she didn't know yet—and none of it good. Like how her mother would get back into Queen Mary's favor, but not lift a finger to try and save Jane.

The whole thing made me even sadder now that Jane seemed less, well, less historic, and more like what she also was: a girl my age.

"I heard your servants, Mistress Ellen and Mistress Tilney—"

"My nurse," she said. "My lady's maid."

"I heard them talking. The first time I saw you."

"What about, pray tell?"

"Your husband." I felt a shiver again from the romance of it. "Sounds like he's crazy about you."

"Crazy?"

"Mad?" I tried.

"Guildford gone mad?"

"No! Mad about *you*. In love. They said he was scratching your name."

"Oh, that!" She flicked her hand dismissively. "Speak no more of Guildford and his dratted scratchings." She slashed the air. "Jane here." Another slash. "And Jane down here beneath it. We barely know each other. We share a bitter turn of fate."

Sure do, I thought. Having parents who would stick you on the throne and then leave you when they heard about Mary coming.

A pulse jumped in her throat. "We shared a bed." She didn't meet my eye. But her tone was *not* romantic. "Jane be his mother's name as well. Mayhap he be thinking of his lady mother."

"But he wouldn't call her *Jane*?"

"Perchance a code? A full-grown lad of seventeen." She laughed. It was musical but did it ever have an edge to it. "Would he not be far too proud to scratch out, 'Mama, Mama'?"

Someone knocked on the door. And knocked again.

Mistress Ellen?

"Jane, are you in there—"

The door swung open.

My door.

8 Quietness (*noun*: peace, amity, reconciliation)

It was a voice I knew so well, but I couldn't quite place it.

"Hey, Jane—"

Blur…

of an arm…

and something…

I couldn't quite—

"Were you having a nap? I didn't mean to wake you up. But you didn't call me."

"Lady…"

"*What?*"

I was sitting, propped against my pillow. "D'I say something?" I shook my head and blinked a few times. A swirl of something filmy, floaty. A glint of red hair. "Is that you, Megan?"

"Yeah."

I drifted off again. Not anywhere. Just drifting.

When I opened my eyes next, Megan was sitting on my desk chair (my mother's old typing chair on wheels). She was wearing a long paisley skirt and a yellow halter top with some kind of gauzy thing over it, and swiveling from side to side with her chin cupped in her hands. I followed dizzily. "Could you stop moving please?"

Her feet, in yellow slouchy socks, were hooked over the chrome legs. How many times did she change clothes these days? Things were clear now. Back in my life again—just in time to see Megan's hand sweep to the floor.

"Hey, what's this little book?"

I bolted upright. It had fallen, face down, open—

She was picking it up by the front cover; I grabbed the back one. "Wait!" I didn't want anyone touching it.

There it hung, in a tug-of-war between us—pages shifting in the air. "It's mine." I came off sounding like a six-year-old, but Meg let go. I tucked the book into my drawer and pushed it shut. "Just something for my project."

"I think I'd better leave." Meg's green eyes flashed, and when she reached for her shoulder bag, her hair swung forward and blocked her features.

"Don't," I said. "Don't go, Meg. Please. You know how grouchy I am when I wake up."

She gave me a hard look, remembering, I suppose, about a thousand sleepovers. "Can't say I ever noticed that." But she put her bag down and started fiddling with something in her pocket.

"I don't blame you for being pissed at me," she said. "I forgot all about the mall. I'm sorry."

It took me a second to even remember. Then it came rushing back.

"Come on, Jane. I *never* forget stuff."

I know that. That's part of the problem. But I forced a smile. "Never mind," I told her. "It's okay."

Her head was tilted now. "You didn't hear your phone?" Wide-eyed and injured looking. It's just me, Meg, I felt like saying. I'm not interested in how cute you are.

Then, "Hey?" I didn't look right at her. "Did my mom let you in?"

"Yeah. She's tearing around down there. Setting the table for some big dinner."

I closed my eyes for a second to still the chaos in my head. Part relief: she'd put a lid on it for sure then, no big binge in full swing. And part rage at how she could do that: rip *my* world apart and then carry on like nothing had happened.

The room was quiet, except for the cawing of a crow outside. A branch rustled by my window. And Megan fiddled with whatever was in the big patch pocket of her skirt, lips nearly twitching from wanting to tell me something.

Well, she'd cut *me* some slack. "You said you had a mystery?"

"Here!" She pulled out a neatly folded paper. "Somebody wrote me a poem."

I opened it and read:

M orning shook me from a dream of her

e merald eyes her diamond-sharp wit. And i am it i am a

g oner i am moonstruck i a lonely guy

a m evanescent. Not so my emotion, undying devotion, my

n otion to weave flowers in her

H air.

"Whoa, Meg." I gave it back.

"Isn't it too hot to handle?" She giggled. "Evanescent—"

"Bubbly?"

"Nope. I had to look it up; it means fleeting. This guy's *very life* is more fleeting than his devotion to"—she crossed her hands over her cleavage—"me."

"Wow. Just like Heathcliff and Catherine."

She laughed, and did a hokey English accent. "And typed in 'iz own 'and."

"So romantic."

"And so anonymous."

"Who do you *think*?"

She smoothed the poem out in her lap. "Well, I was thinking of guys who like me"—she counted them on her fingers—"Tom Kantor, Donnie Wentworth, Wilson, Sayeed…" This was just too much. "Hey, you don't like Tom Kantor, do you?"

I hesitated half a second, then I went with what the other Jane might call the Sin of Pride. "Uh-uh."

"Good. Because I might. And he…" She shrugged.

"Well, yeah." I nodded. "Obviously."

"I told Crisco she had to be wrong. You would have told me if you did. But I'm not sure about him anyhow. He's kind of a smart ass."

I felt a glimmer of hope. "Oh. Do you think?"

"Yeah. But if he wrote me this poem I might be willing to overlook that. I like being adored with such"—she sighed—"articulation."

She swiveled the chair, raised her arms above her head and swayed, back arched and fingers snapping like castanets. The poem fluttered to the floor and she scooped it up.

"Seriously, Watson, we've got to figure this out."

A game we used to play as kids. "Did you smell it?"

"Smell it?"

"Come on, Sherlock. For clues."

She held it to her nose and squinted in concentration.

"Cigarette smoke?" I suggested.

"Uh-uh."

"Hashish?" I said officiously. "Marijuana?"

"Nope."

"Sweat?"

"Yuk!"

"Wet dog smell? Juicy Fruit gum? Identifiable brand of cologne?"

"It smells…it smells like…paper!"

I took the poem from her and held it to the window's light. "No identifying marks," I said. "Did you fold it yourself or did it come that way? Wait—that's it. How'd you get it, anyhow?"

"It was under my door."

"When you got home?"

"No. I saw it there later, when Crisco was leaving."

I swallowed. "*She* have any guesses?"

"She was already gone when I noticed it."

"Before or after Tom arrived?"

"Tom?"

"Kantor. He came to your house."

"No he didn't."

"But he asked me for directions."

"Directions to my house?" Her "emerald eyes" went wide. "When was that?"

I told her, and we looked at each other.

"Aha!" she said, and I forced myself to nod eagerly along with her.

I handed her her poem.

"Tom Kantor." She smiled in satisfaction.

9 Reverb (*verb*: reverberate, re-echo, resound)

Blue on blue. The sweater was spread out on my comforter when I got home from school a few days later. They were both the shade of blue you sometimes see at twilight. You look up and fill up with happiness, but you also get an ache inside. *That* blue.

I ran my fingers from comforter to sweater: satin to soft cotton knit. My favorite—not itchy. It had little holes—diamond-shaped on the sleeves and shoulders and square on the rest. My dark blue camisole would be perfect under it. Sexy. But sort of accidentally so. I held it in front of me at the mirror, and the very faint edging of cobalt jumped out in my mainly gray eyes. Haloes, my mother used to say when I was small.

"Just perfect for my daughter," I could hear her tell the salesgirl, practically radiating Mode One. I could see her gliding through the store, triumphant. But with an anxious little squint in her eye, hoping this would work.

"Damn her." I folded the sweater and tucked it away in my bottom drawer, where my other sweaters suddenly looked second-class. "Damn her." I said it again to my posters. "To hell," I added to the new one from *It Might Get Loud*. She'd given me that after I watched the DVD with her and Dave.

"Screw her," I said to Aslan. (*Narnia?* you're thinking. Well, I could never quite bring myself to take him down.)

The square face on my alarm clock blinked the time, and I blinked back. She couldn't buy my forgiveness. *Not this time. No way.*

Not this time. No way. The words drummed in my head as I padded downstairs, en route to the Haslers' for my Friday night gig. It was a long night stretching ahead—from making dinner for the twins till past 11:00. But Megan would be by. And anyhow, it beat sitting home with Single Mother as Suck-Up, due any minute.

Megan. I came to an abrupt stop on the runner. About-face.

In my room again, I unzipped my backpack and reached into the drawer. I held the sweater against my cheek for a second, then tucked it into my pack on top of my history, my English, my math. Green was the best color for redheads; everyone knew that. But Megan also rocked in blue.

When the clock passed 10:00, I was thumbing through *Elements of Literature* at the Haslers' kitchen table. I was scrunched up at the edge of Sara's social studies project—a salt-and-flour map of British Columbia—and sick to death of studying for Monday's test. Define the difference between plot and theme and *blah blah blah*, while Megan and the rest of the kids in AP English were reading *Anna Karenina*.

I flipped to the index on a sudden hunch, and there it was: time travel, page 223. I turned to it. "A genre of fiction." *Ha! So much for believing what you learn in school.* But the rest of the description seemed true enough: "Time travel is made possible through a portal of some kind, often a key or a secret door which must be opened."

I closed my eyes and pictured the prayer book, with its leather cover. I could see the ornate letters and the drawings around some of them. Illuminated, I now knew it was called. Deep gold. Dusty rose. And indigo. And a soft red that could have been copied from Campbell's cream of tomato soup. I could nearly feel the pages turning, and see Lady Jane's finger tracing a line beneath the words.

It had to be *her* book. Same one I'd caught a glimpse of in her room. I imagined the flowery scent that seemed to float around her—rosewater? And that old-sock smell of cheese. And then the fresh, leafy smell that would have risen from the grass, I figured, after all that rain. But I couldn't go there. Couldn't will myself to *get* there from the Haslers' kitchen, because of what the textbook said next, and I already knew: "Without the portal, no movement through time can occur."

I read the rest of the description and flipped the book shut. It did not, of course, answer my questions. Like, why did the days seem to move twice as fast in that world—whole days, that is? But when it came down to hours and minutes, I couldn't find any pattern, and it seemed to shift around. I could be in the past for one short conversation, but when I got back here whole hours were gone. And vice versa. And then there were my big questions: Why had I been sent there? Was there something I was supposed to do?

What brought me back to my own time—this I *did* get—was when something woke me up here. The phone, or someone calling my name. Or *shaking* me.

I shook my head to knock some sense in—whatever sense was now—and went to fill the kettle. What was keeping Megan? The window above the sink was dark, and my face floating there, reflected, looked as pale as Lady Jane's. The lace trim on the curtains was like the trim on her big sleeves. Things seemed to be echoing, mixing up together. The dress Lady Jane had refused from her cousin, before she became Queen Mary. The sweater I would *not* be bribed with. My name. Our name.

Were *both* of us somehow doomed?

I tugged the curtains shut and went back to the table. Sara's map, on a slab of plywood, claimed most of the space. My English book lay beside it. And, on the other side, my history book was open to a world map, circa Lady Jane's time. "Here Be Dragons," it said for uncharted waters. The world of the unknown.

The bell rang and I scooted down the hall. "Hey, Meg." But another figure stood beside her, nose ring glinting in the porch light.

"Oh." This didn't come out too welcoming.

"Crisco showed up just when I was leaving," Megan burbled. "She's got some great news."

"A job," Crisco said, "at the Black Market."

"She just had the interview today and they called her up already," Megan added. Official Cheerleader for Crisco Dieppe.

"Congratulations," I offered. But my voice came out flat.

Crisco was wearing a black cotton jacket, slumpy, and Converse sneakers over bare feet. With the toe of one, she poked at some early fallen leaves beneath the railing.

"Look, I can go." She glanced up the street as if planning her route.

"No, no, come in." I was suddenly afraid Megan might go with her. "I didn't mean to be rude."

I sort of flapped around while they took their shoes off. "It's just...I don't know how much company they want me to have at one time."

Megan practically glared at me. "How many times have Theresa and I been here together?"

Crisco looked up from unlacing a sneaker. "Theresa who?"

"Well, you've got to know Theresa?" I said. "I mean Traci, our friend."

Crisco looked blank.

"Meg must have mentioned her. She just made the cheer-leading squad? Goes out with Dane MacGregor in grade eleven?"

"Does she ever." Megan rolled her eyes. "They're like Siamese twins." She shrugged. "My old friend, Theresa."

I stepped back as if she'd slapped me. How long before I'd be her old friend, Jane?

The kettle whistled and I escaped into the kitchen. It would be one thing if Meg was *jealous* of Traci and Dane. But Meg? No chance. She just dissed them. Blew them off. That simple.

"Hey, Jane. Have they got any of that good hot chocolate?" she asked as the two of them traipsed in.

Crisco yakked on about the discount she'd be getting at the Black Market—all the cool earrings she'd buy and how she'd do her room up with incense and scarves. "And great to have a real job, instead of looking after someone's brats." She caught my eye and clapped a hand over her mouth. "Sorry!"

Megan took three mugs from their hooks and Crisco wandered around, managing to look sheepish and nosy at the same time.

"Cool map." She ran a finger along the coast where the Rocky Mountains meet the sea. Then she stood at the fridge door and gawked at the twins' school photos. "How can you tell them apart?"

I shrugged.

Her nosiness was a pain, like everything else about her. But I could, reluctantly, see where she was coming from. Like when you go somewhere to babysit for the first time—that moment when the kids are asleep and you're alone in some stranger's rooms like you've been dropped there from outer space: here's an example of a life. I remembered feeling that way a couple of years ago in this same yellow kitchen. *If I ate at this table, had these kids, and went out to dinner and a movie with my husband, who was Mr. Hasler, would that be a good enough life?*

Megan spun from the counter, cupping her mug of chocolate in both hands. Not for her, it wouldn't. She was going to be an international lawyer, and an actor in her spare time.

"Where's the bathroom?" Crisco asked, and I sent her to the one that was farthest away. She headed upstairs, to stick her nose in the medicine cabinet for all I knew. Meg found a bare patch at the table near the US border and sat there sipping, blowing prettily at the steam.

I got my backpack and took the sweater out. "Got something for you. Here." I passed it to her.

"Jane, it's beautiful." She cradled it in both hands. "Why would you give this away?"

"It just looks bad on me."

"This blue? No way."

But I insisted. "Something about how it hangs. Maybe because I don't have any boobs."

"Don't say you—"

"Don't have *much*, I mean. It really doesn't work. My mom bought it," I added, and I didn't have to say the rest: *Don't wear it when you come to my house.* Meg would know. Since the subject had taken a subtle turn from sweater (hers, now) to mother (unavoidably mine), I was actually glad when Crisco sauntered back in.

"Woo-hoo. That woman's got some skimpy black negligee hanging on the bathroom door," she said. "She sexy? Is her husband hot?"

This made me choke on my hot chocolate. "He's bald and he talks with a lisp!" Which was totally true. But the Haslers were nice to me, and I felt guilty when the three of us stopped laughing. *Crisco, you'll never set foot in my house again.* I could see her checking out my mother's scotch supply: "A binger? Or just your regular weekend lush?" I was glad—not for the first time—that my turn to host the peer-editing group was safely done with.

My name was being called. "Ja-a-ne!"

I went to the foot of the stairs. "What is it, Abby?" Probably Crisco's loud laughter had woken her up. I went up to talk to her and get her back to sleep, and when I returned to the kitchen, Meg and Crisco were convulsed in laughter. Meg's arms were crossed over her chest, and her shoulders were shaking. I did a double take. Her shoulders were blue. Didn't even wait for me, to try it on.

"Go on," said Crisco. "Show her!"

"Show me what?"

Meg spread her arms like some girl jumping out of a cake. The smile was dazzling, but what you really saw was the boobs. The sweater was so tight it was like, yeah, here's why they call them headlights.

"Take it off," said Crisco.

Meg hummed a sultry little tune.

"No, not like that! You extrovert."

Meg laughed. "Exhibitionist, you mean?"

"What I *mean* is take it off before you stretch it, then you can't give it to me." She shot a glance in my direction. "Oops."

I just looked down. The eggplant-colored polish was half chipped off her toenails. How impressive.

"Give it to her if you want," I said to Megan. "It doesn't matter to me."

Crisco tugged on the nearest blue sleeve. "Mine!" Not so much as a thank-you in my direction. No acknowledgement from either one of them.

Meg shoved Crisco away with a new burst of giggles. "Stop mauling me, you...extrovert!"

I swirled the lukewarm chocolate in my mug. *Give an example of irony.* That had been another of the questions for Monday's English test. *Where I'm going later, I won't be nearly this invisible.*

10 Queen (*in chess*: the only female piece on the board, and the most powerful)

"Fie!" Lady Jane's queen swept across the board and killed another of my pawns, then settled ominously on the square beside my bishop.

I'd landed in Jane's room again—her and me and Mistress Ellen, who was sewing by the window. I glanced over; it still freaked me out that she couldn't see me. Her needle was making a loop, darting through a patch of sunlight.

Daytime here. Back at home, Mr. Hasler's forehead had gleamed beneath the streetlight when he dropped me off.

"Would it be time you made a move?" Jane whispered, and I started to whisper back then remembered *I* didn't have to. "Forthwith." *Cool word.* "Just wait until forthwith," I told her. A little army of casualties was scattered between us on the bed. The pawns were like miniatures of Columbus's ships. The whole set—borrowed from the Partridges—was amazing. A few fallen pieces had rolled out of sight beneath the folds of Jane's skirts. Silk today. Deep olive.

I started to move my bishop to safety, but saw something better—and moved a pawn instead. My queen would now have a clear path to kill Jane's queen *if* she took my bishop. Any chance she wouldn't see that? I looked down, avoiding her eyes. But I could feel them on me—shrewd, and especially prominent-looking today, set off by a brown velvet headdress with a band of bright gold stitching.

"Your bishop as a sacrifice?" she whispered. "Do you take me for a fool?"

"No. That's what *you* keep taking *me* for."

"I can hear you," Mistress Ellen said, and I think my heart stopped.

But it was her lady she was speaking to. "Wouldst that your tutors could visit, or I could play the game myself." She *tsk*ed. "Chattering to your ownself like a magpie."

"A far sight better than croaking like a Tower raven."

The nurse snorted. "'Tis true." She put her sewing down and came over, leaning over my side of the board. So close, I could feel puffs of air when she breathed out.

Jane smiled. "Do you recall the time I beat my cousin when we visited her at Hampstead?"

"And you but a child, how could I not?" She straightened up, hands on her hips, and I let myself expand again.

"How we played until our ladies fell to sleeping in their chairs?"

"And fresh candles had to be sent for."

Jane was rolling one of my casualties around in her palm. A castle. Narrow, tall, with slim, round turrets. She looked up at her nurse with a mischievous grin. "And do you believe Her Grace is reaping now her vengeance?"

Mistress Ellen stepped back. "Watch your tongue, my lady."

"Wherefore? There be no one here"—Jane's eye caught mine and moved on—"save the two of us."

"Take care no ear be pressed against the door before you

speak so rashly. That would be my counsel. Ach!" She waved a hand. "Mind not. These dark days soon shall pass. Once Her Grace declares your pardon, you and she may once again—"

"Say not." Jane closed her fist around the castle. "Some things cannot again…grow cozy. I shall no more pass an evening with the Papist queen than I shall walk again"—she drew a breath—"with Edward Seymour."

I knew that name, her "first betrothed," who the biographies said she might have been in love with. No "might have" about it. You could tell from that sharp intake of breath.

"Think not on what is lost, my lady. Go back to practicing your game. 'Twas putting you in fine good cheer." Mistress Ellen reached down and plucked the pawn I'd just moved. She rubbed her thumb along the full slope of its sails, then put it back—on the wrong square.

"I must needs cross the Green," she said, "to fetch a spool of good strong thread to mend your cloak. Trusting that one of Her Grace's fine ladies will see fit"—she gave a sniff—"to spare one for the likes of us now."

Jane looked at her. "My ermine-lined?"

She nodded. "It be November, after all. I can feel it in my bones, the coming-on of winter." *November—it sounded right if time was moving twice as fast here.* She rubbed her arms and closed her pale blue eyes, letting a shiver run through her. Then she looked again—too soon: I was sliding my pawn back.

"Dear Lord! I could have sworn that piece just mo…mine eyes are playing tricks on me"—she shook her head—"from too much time in consort with the needle."

Once she was gone, Jane leaned across the chessboard. "I pray you are *not* a spy of some manner?"

"A spy who happens"—I waved a hand to where Mistress Ellen had been standing—"to be invisible?"

"A spy...from above?"

This took me a second. Then, "Come on," I said. "Is there any such thing as spies from heaven?"

"Not by my reckoning, but"—her brown eyes searched my features—"be there any such thing as *you*?"

I offered her my hand, like *here I am*. She didn't take it. It must have freaked her out, of course, how real I *was* to her. I turned it palm down and spread my fingers, looking between them at the black-and-white world of the chessboard. "Why would God have to send a spy anyhow? Can't he see everything?"

I think her eyes sent sparks out. "If you have come to test my faith, let me assure you it is impeccable."

Why would I test *her* faith, when *I* didn't have one? That's what I nearly said but caught myself. People like me were called heretics here. Burned at the stake. Or, on a good day, just dragged through the streets and whipped, naked.

"I didn't mean to..." What could I say? "I come to be your friend, my lady."

"There be precious few friends in the Tower of London."

"All the more reason you need one."

We sat there looking at each other. On her scratchy blanket, with the chessboard and the fallen pieces.

Then she gave a funny little smile—her bemused-but-humoring-me smile. "What would you *be*, in this," she paused, "this 'time and place' you speak of? Perchance a noblewoman?" She looked strangely at my jeans and top, not for the first time. "I cannot fathom your standing."

"I'm a commoner."

"Oh. Are you a...spinner, mayhap? An apothecary?"

"I go to school."

"A school for *girls*? For *commoners*?"

"Yeah. Girls and boys. Everyone goes."

She laughed out loud, then tried another angle: "Are you wed?"

"I'm not even sixteen."

"*I* be just shy of sixteen. Are you betrothed?"

"No, we don't..." How to explain how we did things? "Well, there is this guy I like."

"A man named Guy?"

"A boy, named Tom. But he likes my friend." First time I'd said it out loud. Well, my secret could hardly be safer.

I don't remember what got us back to our chess game. Maybe we needed something where we knew the rules already. Jane did kill my bishop, but with her horse instead of her queen—how had I managed not to see that? Then I did see an unprotected square beside her king. I could get my queen there in two moves and—checkmate! My castle was in line already, riding shotgun.

My next move got her halfway there, and I was scared to take my finger off her smooth little ivory crown. I kept checking and rechecking the board for danger. "I'm nearly useless if my queen gets killed." Then I clapped my hand over my mouth, à la Crisco. "Sorry!"

Jane looked confused.

Oh, *right*. I would never have apologized if I didn't know her future. Or lack of one. "Um, it just seemed like a rude thing to say, since you just *were* a queen."

"Not at all," she reassured me. "You are but a pawn, from what you say." She gestured at the fallen pieces. "We have both killed a number of your kind."

Whoa. "I've never thought of myself quite like that."

I heard her take a breath. "Have I offended you?"

I wasn't ready to meet her eyes.

"I have spoken far too bold. As I am wont to do. Prithee, I cry thee mercy. I be most unaccustomed to speaking with commoners."

Or travelers through time. I had to give her that. I smiled, and she sighed with relief.

Then she laughed. It was her edgy laugh.

"What?" I said.

She snatched her queen from the board, and a pawn, and held them out to me. "I have been both. And at the self-same hour."

11 Misconster (*verb*: misconstrue, take wrongly)

For the next couple of weeks, you'd have thought *Crisco Dieppe* was queen—not just a cashier-in-training. Cool boss and "can't wait for my paycheck" and *blah blah blah*. "Like she's special," I muttered to Traci at our lockers one afternoon. "It's just that she turned sixteen before the rest of us."

"Early birthday?" Traci pulled her backpack higher on her shoulders as we headed for the Bell Road door. "Or maybe she flunked a year?"

I tapped her arm in appreciation. "Ha!"

Traci was wrapped up in her cheerleading—not to mention Dane. And me? I couldn't tell anyone what *I* was up to. Lots of visits to the other Jane. Once, when I arrived, she was holding the *Booke of Prayre*. The cover was brighter, the dark red somehow clearer. It practically glowed.

"Would you like to see?" She had noticed me staring.

My hand shot out, but then came back again as if on its own accord. I shook my head. I remembered how she had shied away from taking my hand once—a couple of times. That's how I felt about the book. In her world, it might be dangerous to touch.

In my world, I was watching Megan bat her eyelashes at Tom. *My Life As A Muse*—she had declared on Facebook. If it *was* him, why hadn't he made a move by now?

One day she and I were kicking back in her room (which is gorgeous; the whole attic of her house). Meg was sitting on her bed and I was stretched out on the carpet, under one of her *three* skylights, while we worked on our history projects—though Meg was mostly texting Crisco. Slow shift at the Black Market, it seemed. All three of us were speculating about Tom.

"Why don't you just ask him out yourself?"

She gave me a look so close to pity that I flinched. "It's like a dance we're doing, Jane. Don't you get that? Don't you know the steps?"

Maybe they could both call me "kid." Crisco too. All three of them.

"Hey, do you think he's scared of me?" She dropped her phone onto her pillow.

"He's hardly a wimp."

"No. But remember how Donnie Wentworth said I was intimidating?"

I scrunched up a piece of paper and threw it at her. "Megan! Get over yourself. I'm trying to concentrate on"— I glanced at the web page that was open on my laptop— "Courtly Customs of the Early Renaissance."

She gave a back-to-schoolwork sigh. "Find anything good?"

I shrugged, then closed my eyes and recited something I knew from Jane:

"If on your man you light,
The first draught you may play.
If not 'tis mine by right
At first to leade the way.

"They say that at the start of a chess game. She hides one piece in each fist—or he, I mean—and the other person picks one."

"And you've got it memorized? God, you're a nerd," she said affectionately, then tossed an eraser, which boinged off my head.

She flipped her binder open. "Listen. I mean: Hear ye this!"

I rolled onto my back and stared up at a sliver of moon— the sky was just darkening—while I listened to Meg read a poem in an uppity English accent. Some guy called Thomas Wyatt had written it for Anne Boleyn.

"I had to go on a database at Dalhousie to find it."

I sat up. *"Who's* a nerd?"

"I know." She laughed. "But doesn't it just make you shiver?"

"Well, to tell you the truth it seemed a little stiff."

She shot me a look of exaggerated patience. "I *mean,* the fact that Anne Boleyn was getting poems written to her. Like me."

I groaned.

"And at the same time that I'm studying her? It makes me feel like we're connected somehow"—she was cross-legged, gathering her hair into a ponytail—"through time." She dipped her chin while she twisted the elastic on. "Wish I could go back in time."

The moon above the skylight was the slimmest paring of a nail. *Could she possibly be trying to…tell me…?* I realized I was gripping the pile of the carpet.

"It *did* make you shiver! You've got goosebumps. Look."

Form every word with care. Sound normal. "You said. You wanted to go back. In time?"

"Uh-huh. And warn her. I read she loved this guy. Not the poem guy. Another"—she waved a hand, airily—"admirer. But her family broke it up. They were real shits, one thing Anne and I *don't* have in common. They make my parents look great, in spite of"—she pouted—"my miniscule allowance."

Meg's parents were gems and we both knew it. Sometimes she had even tried to share them, saying I should move in. This went back to grade eight, when she'd noticed (though I'd tried to hide it) that my mom had been missing in action for two days.

"Meg." I couldn't help myself. "To go back in ti—to go back and warn her. It would only upset her for nothing, don't you think? You couldn't go back and actually change what happened?"

She did a double take. "Perhaps if you believe in some theory of parallel universes." She frowned at me. "Jane? I didn't mean that literally. I may be a drama queen—you know I am—but I'm not out of touch with reality."

I flopped down on my back again so she couldn't get a look at my embarrassed face. There were no stars through the skylight, just the moon up there, alone.

In the next day's history class, Mr. Gregor passed around some books with portraits of the Tudors and unrolled a poster: Cate

Blanchett as Elizabeth I. She looked determined, almost scary. But as a couple of the girls pointed out, the gorgeous red hair streaming over her shoulders looked a lot like Megan's.

"She had a long reign," Mr. Gregor was saying, "and became known as Good Queen Bess. She had charisma."

"And good hair," said Stella. Then she blushed when people snickered.

"Why, thank you," Megan said with a giggle, and Mr. Gregor ran a hand through his own hair—an indistinct, ashy shade. "I'm glad we've got our priorities straight. But that *does* bring up a point about historical accuracy," he said. "Can someone tell me what's wrong with this picture? What might be false?"

I raised my hand. "She would have been wearing a head-dress?"

"Right, or something like it. A woman's hair uncovered—it just wasn't thought proper."

Probably half the class turned then and looked at Yasmeen, in her softly draped, fawn-colored hijab. She smiled, chin cupped in her palm.

Crisco raised a hand. "But hair's important too. I mean in history." Her spiky cut was freshly dyed a mustard color, making her skin even more ghoulish. "Like what happened to Samson, in the Bible—"

"That isn't *history*," Tom said, and I think Mr. Gregor could have kissed him: "Super! A debate for another day."

Crisco cut back in. "Don't people say Elizabeth's red hair was a sign of her fiery temper?"

"You mean like Megan's?" This was Simon Wong. "She nearly took my head off today in Chemistry."

Meg raised her binder and went to swat him across the aisle. "He was snooping through my notes!"

"I was looking for a formula—"

Mr. Gregor rattled Cate Blanchett. "We're not here to talk about formulas. Or whether Ms. Hollingsworth has an Elizabethan temper." Megan folded her arms beneath her breasts. "As well she might."

The door swung open then, and Steve Ripley and the other two guys on the football team came strolling in from their Thursday morning practice. Ripley cuffed the others on the shoulder with a beefy fist, and they headed for their seats. We all waited. Even Mr. Gregor, no fan of interruptions, seemed frozen in a moment of respect.

I glanced at Tom and saw something that floored me: envy. His head was tilted down but his eyes were on the football players. Jealous eyes—*a not-so-athletic guy trying to imagine what it must be like?* My heart went out. Then, all of a sudden, his eyes were on me; we both looked away. Had he seen me noticing? And, worse yet, feeling bad for him? I looked again. Him too. I made a face. I-didn't-see-anything-why-are-you-looking-at-me?—that's what I was aiming for. But I knew it came out like why-are-*you*-looking-at-*me*?

He scowled back.

One of Mr. Gregor's books landed on my desk and I stuck my stupid face in that. Was it *football* he wanted? Not the game itself, I figured. The status? Or—well, everyone knew the same rumors—girls lined up to do whatever the football team might like.

I tried to focus on the book. The portrait with Jane's name beneath it wasn't Jane at all, but some dour-looking woman about thirty. I skimmed the other royals and their friends—Sir Thomas Cromwell, Thomas More, Sir Walter Raleigh, who had a famous crush on Elizabeth I.

Megan, I should tell you out of fairness, never looked pinched or haughty like Elizabeth in her portraits. Or mean-eyed like Cate Blanchett in that poster. But Tom took the look-alike hair thing and ran with it, finally making his move.

"Hail to the Queen!" he said the next time Meg gave an opinion on some question, and Mr. Gregor raised an eyebrow.

"Does this display of fealty have any bearing on our class discussion?"

Stella and Alexa spun their sleek blonde heads around in unison, and Meg's next comment was dynamite: "Who speaketh? Is that Sir Walter Raleigh?" She cracked everyone up.

Mr. Gregor brought the class back to order. And I spent the last few minutes before the bell rang just trying to contain the heavy feeling in my chest. Tom and Megan. Looked like it was really going to happen. TK ♥ MH. And I'd get to hear every juicy detail.

I escaped as soon as the big minute hand jerked forward to twenty minutes past. But not fast enough to miss Tom heading over to our side of the room, making a beeline to where Megan was standing, waiting, at her desk.

Things didn't unfold as expected.

I had just dried the supper dishes that night and was putting them away when Megan phoned.

"He kept going on with the Walter Raleigh thing. Tom *can* go on."

My stupid heart did another flip of empathy.

"He said he'd spread his cloak out if we came to any mud puddles."

"Yeah, like Raleigh." I closed the cupboard door and looked out the back window to the lane. "So you could step on it."

"I know. That was in some old movie. But how thick could a cloak be? Wouldn't her feet still get wet?"

"I guess it was more a symbol, a sign of his admiration."

"That's what Tom said. *Yada, yada.* So I said, 'that's all well and good…'"

I could hear the smile in her voice, hear her savoring the memory.

"'…like a sign of *devotion*,' I said…"

I thought of Timbit, the cat we used to have—how I'd once seen her batting some poor mouse around.

"…and I said it *just like that.* With a capital D, Jane. And there wasn't a flicker of recognition. It wasn't him who wrote me that poem."

"Are you sure?" This was my attempt to hide my hopefulness. "Maybe he was just, you know, bluffing. Trying to play it cool?"

"I wondered that too. So I went even further."

Mrs. Lynde's Toyota rumbled by—a splash of red between the gray boards of the fence—while I waited for what Meg would say next.

"'But is it evanescent?' I asked. And he just looked at me, like, What in hell are you talking about? 'Your *devotion*, is it *evanescent*?'" She laughed. "I must have sounded like a space cadet. Then, oh," she hesitated, "Jane…"

This would clearly be the painful bit.

"...he said, 'Well, you want me to be...*bubbly*? I can be bubbly.'"

"*No!*"

"I felt so bad for him."

Me too.

"He wasn't bluffing."

"No. No way." Even though I hardly knew him, it was like I'd always known him. Even the annoying parts. "Tom Kantor," I said, "would never pretend to get something wrong."

I slipped my phone into my pocket and practically skipped up the stairs. It wasn't him, thank god. *Thank you god for that much. I won't have to watch them all over each other.* I almost bumped into my mom coming down with both arms around the laundry basket. She swayed back to balance things, and I could just see her face over some towels and the puffy corner of a fitted sheet.

She caught my eye. "You're looking chipper."

"Oh? I guess."

"Get a good mark on your math test?"

"There's more to life." Would she ever let up?

"I'm sorry, sweetie. Of course there is."

I was squeezing past her now. She breathed a big breath up, to blow a strand of hair from her eyes. It was freshly washed, and shining. "Jane, I haven't"—she hesitated—"seen you wear that sweater."

"No, I know, Mom. I like it, like I told you. But I'm saving it for something special."

"Oh." Her voice was small, but then she tried again. "Are you busy, sweetie? I was thinking, after I throw this in, maybe a game of chess? It's been a long time."

"Thanks, but no." I tried to look regretful.

"Scrabble?"

I kind of *felt* regretful. "Sorry, Mom. Lots of homework."

In my room, I shut the door behind me. Not a slam. Slams were echoes of Mode Three; they made me nervous. I liked just the click of a boundary between us.

I took the prayer book from its drawer, and turned the soft, cream-colored pages to Psalm 51.

Have mercy upon me O God,
according to thy loving-kindness:

You could sort of call this homework…

12 Aroint (found only in the imperative mood: "get thee gone")

She was sitting by the window with a book open in her lap. "*J'espère.*" I cocked my head so I could hear her better. "*J'espérerai. J'aurai espéré…*"

Her hands were bare, one finger following the words. It seemed as if her nails were chewed down more each time I saw them. How sure was she feeling about that pardon? Was it just coincidence that she was conjugating "hope"?

I leaned over to unsnag my sock from a splinter in the rough-plank floor, and when I looked up again she'd seen me.

"Namesake!" She smiled like I was her best friend.

Probably true.

She was wearing her olive green dress again—heavy silk, with brocaded sleeves. Like all her dresses, it had a stiff-looking front that tapered down to a V-shape, and then the full skirt split open to show an equally full inner layer—her "chemise"—this one dark green.

She put her French book on top of a stack she had made on the floor. Ancient history? Philosophy?

She followed my eye. "'Tis a blessing I have leave to keep them."

"Can I take a look?"

"Prithee, do."

I thought of Meg and me and all the books that we've devoured. No *Anne* or *Harry Potter* or *Hunger Games* here. I pulled out one with a blue leather cover.

"If only my tutor could come to help with my studies." She shook her head.

"There's no way he can?"

She looked exasperated. "Mr. Aylmer be of the New Faith."

"Sorry!" What was I thinking? Her tutors, whom she'd always loved, had all been Protestant. The Catholic queen would hardly let one of them visit her here.

I propped the book on the wide stone windowsill and we leaned into it together. The paper was soft like in the prayer book, but these pages were large—every one I turned cut a temporary slash across the Green. People were milling around down there, more than I'd ever seen before. In the book, something was wrong. The letters were the same—swirls, tails, etcetera—but the words weren't making sense.

"What *is* this, anyway?"

"'Tis Latin." Then, with a hint of laughter in her voice: "Do they not teach Latin in that school you spoke of?"

"No," I admitted. "But they do teach"—what would impress her?—"html. At least I think they do. It's a language used for writing on...machines."

"On printing presses?"

"No. Way different. Faster." What would she make of e-books? Or Google? "*I* could tutor you," I said. "If you'd like, I mean."

"Do you know Greek?" Her expression was doubtful. "Would you be well-versed in *The Iliad*?"

"Well, no."

She tried again. "Or ciphering?"

"My ciphering isn't so good."

"Too bad."

Too bad? I did a double take. She must have gotten that from me, like I had to catch myself at home sometimes from saying "verily" or "'tis."

She sighed. Me too. A universal language.

I went to close the book, but took a second glance at the title page—the only one with a picture. It was a drawing of an island. Wooden ships sailed around it, like the pawns in the Partridges' chess set and the Tall Ships that sailed into Halifax Harbour for festivals. A sea monster spurted away.

There was one word in big letters across the top: VTOPIAE.

Wait a minute. "I think I've heard of this book."

"Verily?"

"This"—I tapped the island—"is *Utopia?*"

She nodded. "By Sir Thomas More."

I didn't know if Sir Thomas *Kantor* was even speaking to me right now, after our little scowling contest. But if only I could bring him here. *Take a look at this.*

"He was a Papist, Thomas More." Jane's mouth turned down. "Mr. Aylmer sayeth he had fine ideas nonetheless, so I be at a loss to argue." She ran a finger down the page. "He *did* go to the scaffold for his faith, misguided though it be. I give him that. He did not betray his God to save his own mean flesh, as many do."

But they survive, I thought. *The ones who betray their gods. They don't get their heads cut off for nothing.*

I took a breath. "And *you.* If you turned Catholic—Papist— would they let you out of here?"

She gasped. And when she spoke again she didn't look at me.

"Her Grace my cousin shall release me when all threat is gone. God willing she forgive me." She threw her hands up, clearly aggravated. "First, she must have no fear that a rebel army might rise up to bring the New Faith back, by putting me, once again, on her throne. Can you not see that?"

"Yes. But if you *did* turn Papist, publicly I mean, then they *couldn't* put you there."

"Nay. 'Twould make no sense to."

"*See?* You *don't* have to put your whole life on the line." She was backing away from me.

I could save her. I suddenly got it. Because I saw things in a way she couldn't. *That's* why the book was sent to me. And why I had been sent here. I just had to convince her.

"It's all the same, my lady. All one god."

She backed farther away.

"If there's a chance someone could save themselves—for sure, I mean, and right now—shouldn't they take it?" I was keeping pace with her. I think I was waving my hands around for emphasis. We circled the room.

"You are saying I should betray my Holy Father if it would help secure my pardon!"

"I am not," I said. Then, "*Yeah*. Thing is, it doesn't matter. We know that now. We know that where I come from."

The air went out of her like I'd kicked her in the stomach.

"Then where you come from is a Godless place. And what, pray, does that make *you*?"

But I kept on trying. "You could just pretend. You wouldn't have to mean—"

"*Pretend*?" She stood her ground now, glaring. "*Pretend* to worship at the Papist altar? *Pretend* to give confession to some over-stuffed, glass-gazing priest who would place himself between my conscience and my Lord. There are those who would pretend such things. This Court"—she flung an arm out—"it be rife with them." Her voice tapered to a whisper. "How could you count me in that number?"

Then she stamped a boot heel. "Leave me. Leave me now."

"I—what?"

"I bid thee farewell, Namesake."

"I can't," I said. "I can't leave here even if I wanted to…" I let my voice trail off. She was standing by the window now, and I could see how flushed her cheeks were. How hard her jaw was clenched.

"I believed you were my friend." She stared out at the Green. "My friend…I knoweth not the words: my…miracle." Her eyes narrowed as she turned to look at me. "But you came here to lead me astray. You are an instrument of the Devil—"

"Wait—" I started.

"A doer of evil, an imp."

"No. Don't *say* that!"

What she called me next was even worse.

I slammed the door of her measly little prison room behind me and headed down the stairs. A steep stone staircase with no railing. I ran my hand along the wall and something pricked my finger. I sucked on it. Salty taste of blood. Then I shoved the door open, stepped out, and got walloped by—

Mistress Tilney. She'd come barreling at me—didn't feel me at all, it seemed; just plowed right through. I howled,

from being hit by her bony elbows and kicked in the shin by
her boot.

The Green was full of people, and I hobbled along among
them—on high alert, keeping out of their way.

Were they peasants? Were they workers, going home for
the night? Where *were* they all going? A little kid scampered
by with a piglet in his arms; I couldn't tell which one was
squealing. A man in a leather apron loomed in front of me.
Sharp tools dangled from his belt and he had a smudge like
charcoal on one cheek, but his eyes were kind. I veered away
so he wouldn't trample me. I saw a staircase carved into the
Tower wall, and ran for it.

I wound my way up and around, up and around, and came
out on top. I took a breath, and took another one; my lungs
felt like sandpaper. I looked back over the edge. The Green
was dizzyingly far below.

I was alone except for one man—a guard marching back
and forth. He wore a red tunic, black stockings, and a floppy
red hat. I tucked myself into a corner, out of his path. I curled
up there until my heartbeat slowed. Until it faded into a softer,
steady thumping, in rhythm with his boot heels on the stone.

He stopped sometimes and looked out through the ramparts. Out to the other side. I got up after a bit, on shaky legs,
and joined him.

The moat was a muddy green. It was way below us, but
it sent up a smell like when you open an outhouse door. I
took my next few breaths just through my mouth. Beyond the
moat, the rooftops of London: a few wide streets and lots of
narrow ones, and twisting lanes and rickety alleys that looped
their way down to the Thames.

It was full of boats, the Thames. Tall ships, majestic. Rowboats. Lumpy-looking barges. And there were nicer-looking barges that reminded me a bit of Viking ships.

The bridge that crossed the river was lined with houses, like a street. A shiver went through me. London Bridge. The famous one—from the nursery rhyme, I mean. Except it *wasn't* falling down. Unlike much of the city, the bridge looked proud and sturdy, with its houses four stories high and taller. Smoke from their chimneys streamed into the sky.

The sun was sinking while I stood there in silent company with the guard. A pinkish glow hung over London.

A chill came up, but then it seemed to float right off me, like the pain had after my crash with Mistress Tilney. Weird. And now that I thought of it, I *should* be cold. November here, and I didn't have a jacket.

I held my finger up—and couldn't find the cut. All healed, already? I checked the other hand. No, this was the right hand. What *was* this? If I got hurt here...if I got *killed* here, would I really die?

I tried to push the thought away. The sky was getting darker. Now I could hardly see my hands in front of me. I was ready for my phone to ring. For anything—my mother even, please—to reach through time and get me, call me home.

But I was still there when a new guard came to replace the first guy. He brought a lantern with him, a burning stump of rope in a rusty cage. It threw most of its light back on him, showing me his bulbous nose and pitted cheeks, and the smoke from it tickled my throat. This new guard seemed to find the night as long as I did. He kept taking swigs from a flask. Then he'd smack his scabby lips and spit down into the moat.

When I peeked out now, I could hardly see the city. London was a blanket—probably scratchy like my lady's, who I was trying not to think about. It was dotted here and there with sparks. A church bell rang, and rang again, again. Or had it turned into an echo? A voice called out. I strained to pick out the words. It was a single voice. Clear, repeating. Coming closer, and carrying over the wall:

"Remember the clocks,
Look well to your locks,
Fire and your light,
And God give you good night,
For now the bell ringeth."

13 Alarumed (*adjective*: galvanized, activated, stirred to action)

From the sea of people streaming past next morning, Steve Ripley came looming out.

"Smile, Lady Jane, your face won't crack." He stretched his own features in an exaggerated grin. "Lose your best friend?"

I sure felt like it. But she wasn't far behind him. My real best friend. She was threading her way toward Traci and me with one hand clutching something to her chest, and the other high above the crowd and waving.

We nearly got smashed into a bank of lockers.

"What's that?" Though I could see by now it was a yellow notebook.

"It's the answer!" she crowed. "Here. Yours for safekeeping." She foisted it on me and wrapped her arms around the two of us, spinning us in a tight little dance that set Traci's ponytail swinging.

"I snooped through Simon's chem notes like he was snooping through mine," she whispered. "Voila! Take a look."

When I got to French I opened my binder, slipped Simon Wong's notebook inside where Madame wouldn't notice, and started thumbing through. Lots of formulas that meant zilch to me. No hearts with Megan's name, if that's what I was looking for. Do guys even *do* stuff like that?

Then, on the second-last page:

C oolest of subjects
H elp! Being lacerated
E nervated by lamest of teachers
M y eyes have seen yet
I n years of
S chool cruel
T oo many fools but
R edhead across the aisle, whoa—finest thing in room o
Y eah.

"*Mademoiselle Grey, avez-vous une réponse pour question numéro trois?*"

"Forthwi—" *God*. I flipped through my binder. "*Un moment, s'il vous plaît.*"

"I don't like it as much as the first one, though." Meg dug into the cookie jar.

No surprise. Being the "finest thing in room" was cool, but likely a comedown from "undying devotion" less "evanescent" than life itself. I personally didn't know.

"The double meaning of 'chemistry''s neat."

She frowned. Then, "Hey, I didn't *get* that. Pretty good, Jane. This one's burnt." She held a cookie out and I reached for it. Meg's mom would always have a soft spot for me, she said, because I liked her burnt ones best.

"And it's just what he was doodling in class," Meg continued. "Not even his strongest work."

I laughed. "Sounds like you're talking about Ernest Hemingway. Or Tolstoy."

"Wordsworth." She sniffed. "Or Allen Ginsberg. You could at least get the genre straight."

"*Excusez-moi, ma'm'selle.*" I waved my cookie in the air. "I prefer the peanut butter genre over the chocolate chip."

I bit into the best part, where the prongs of the fork make imprints like rows in a garden, like…frown lines in an old nurse's forehead. Mistress Ellen—now practically her only friend? I gripped the cool metal rim of the table and told myself to focus. *You Are Here.* In Megan's kitchen with the blue and white tiles, and the earthenware jar that's been here since the beginning of *this* particular moment in time.

Where were we? Right. I said, "It sure proves it was him."

"Well, yeah. I can't believe I never noticed he liked me. I can usually tell these things. And I can't believe we didn't think of it before, his poetic sensibility. *Poe.* How did we miss a clue like that one?"

It wasn't the first time she had marveled at this. Or, I figured, the last.

"I can't believe how excited you are. Simon Wong. I mean, Simon who ran crying for his mother the first day of kindergarten. I'll never forget it, how the teacher ran after him and all of us were looking out the window—"

"Ancient history, Jane. You know I didn't move here till grade two."

"But grade three," I said. "His Etch A Sketch. How he

brought it to school every day and didn't he…take it out for
recess? I think he had a name for it, Megan—"

"Maurice."

"Huh?"

"What he called his Etch A Sketch." Her eyes took on a
dreamy look. "I was trying all last period to remember, and
I finally did."

"That's right." I took a nibble and kept watching her.
"Doesn't bother you?"

"I think"—she raised a finger, chewing daintily—"the
early sign of a creative spirit."

"Spare me."

"But seriously, Jane, don't you think he's improving with
age?"

"Well, seriously…"

Open your mind and let go of all your preconceptions. That's
what my mom always told her students to do when they were
deciding if they liked a work of art. And, admittedly, she had
her moments.

Simon Wong. Long and lean, with the tips of his new
hairdo lit like match heads. Those rabbity front teeth. But
there was more. I closed my eyes and saw slim, tapered fingers
moving while he talked, heard the low tones of his voice and
a kind of precision—saying every word right to the end. I saw
the planes of his face as he bent over his notebook, writing
poems to Megan.

I reached for one more cookie. "Seriously. Maybe your
love isn't *all* blind."

When I got home my mother was blasting her music—one of her vintage Bob Dylan CDs. She was hunched over the butcher block, chopping the humungous zucchini Mrs. Lynde had left on our doorstep, same as every fall.

"Spaghetti tonight!" She had to shout it.

I shrugged. Did she think I was some little kid who'd get all excited about a favorite meal? And wasn't it the teenager who was supposed to crank the volume up? Like wasn't it the teenager who was supposed to be a problem? What chance would I ever get?

I headed for the stairs, but Dylan, well, he takes me back. It was so long since I'd heard this cut, it was like some long-lost relative—one we didn't even have—had come to visit. I found myself swaying along to the harmonica, and when it ended with that funny line about how the vandal took the handle, my mother caught my eye. *The vandal lit the candle!* *The vandal ate my sandal!* I remembered us trying to outdo one another, her and me and my dad.

It was like someone had flipped a switch. Next thing I knew I was setting up my English homework right there at the kitchen table (Mode Two, Nothing Day, veering in the direction of Mode One). Bob was turned down to a low roar, accompanied by the sizzling of onions, and a mingling of olive oil and garlic teased at my nose while I answered some questions on *The Old Man and the Sea*.

Like Hemingway, I'd said, and Meg had named some poets. *"Not his strongest work."* A giggle slipped out, and my mom looked over, her eyes widening in anticipation.

Guess who Megan likes? I nearly said. And guess who's writing poems to her? I could imagine her response: *Little*

Simon with his Etch A Sketch. But I bit my tongue and focused on my homework sheet.

When I looked up next, she'd dumped the vegetables into the pot and was wiping down the cutting board, her mouth set, a little hurt. All these unspoken things. Our house was full of them. Like what I was thinking right now: Will you go get some help? *Will you please please get some help?*

"Did you say something, honey?"

"No." *Surely I hadn't talked out loud?*

I was sick of reality slipping around, like a piece of soap you're trying to get hold of in the bathwater. And I knew it was my "traveling" that was doing it—messing with my head. Well, that was over. I flinched, remembering what a sick thing Jane had called me: *"Spawn of Satan!"* I'd never be going there again.

Dylan had launched into the chorus of "Mr. Tambourine Man," and I tried to let his voice fill my head. The pot lights in the ceiling cast a soft glow on the countertop with its Cuisinart and microwave, and the stainless steel fridge. Only the woodstove, on its raised brick hearth, had much in common with the world of five hundred years ago. That and the floor with its black and white tiles—like a chessboard, and like the floors in paintings by Mom's favorite old-time artist, a Dutch painter, Vermeer.

Mom had done all this—put in a whole new kitchen—after my dad's accident, when the first of the insurance money came. I was eight, and I'd hated her for it. There was one fight where I remember screaming, "Blood money! Blood money!" My poor mother; what TV show did I get that from? Later, I'd padded down to the kitchen and found her chopping vegetables, like tonight, but she was hacking at them, pulp and bits flying all over. Her cheeks were wet, and she was swearing, using words she never used back then—and my father's name mixed in.

That's when she told me…everything. And some of the comments I'd overheard suddenly made sense. He had betrayed her. It still hurts me too much to say how. I promised myself then that I'd never do that. I'd protect my mom from people whispering, and from people she couldn't trust. And I'd never, ever put that kind of pain on someone's face.

"My friend…I knoweth not the words: my…miracle."

It was Jane's face now that I was picturing. What *was* I? Just one more betrayal in her tragic life?

Whether I could save her or not, I surely hadn't been sent through time just so two girls could end up in some big blow-up.

"How long till supper, Mom?"

She gave the sauce a stir, considering. "An hour."

I forced a yawn. "Think I'll take a nap."

"That sounds like a good idea, dear. You look like you hardly slept last night."

"Gee, thanks." But I gave her a smile. You'd look tired too, I wished I could have said to her—to *anyone*—if you'd been stuck there with that creepy guard until your alarm went off this morning.

On the way upstairs I nearly changed my mind—again. The very act of climbing steps made me feel like I was going to find ramparts, and a smelly moat, and no way to get out of there. But these stairs were wood, not stone. Our dark green runner down the middle. And I'd be called home soon; I could count on that. Called home for my mother's spaghetti.

14 Metal of India (*noun*: pure gold)

Odin or one of his buddies saw me first. "*Che-ow! Che-ow!*"

Jane was turning in a circle, while three of them flapped around her as she scattered crusts of bread. She had a cloak on—charcoal-colored, trimmed with fur so white that it looked startling in the drab surroundings. Dark-bellied clouds hung low in the sky, and there was a crumbly wall of ruins behind her. A part of the Tower I'd never seen before. Any minute and she—*yes*—her hand stayed frozen in the air.

She'd seen me.

She was holding an egg now and one raven leapt up to snatch it, hiding Jane's face. But I could hear her voice above the jealous "*Caulk! Caulk! Caulk!*"-ing of the other birds, and through the *whoosh* of feathers. "You have come again."

Was it a welcome? Or an accusation?

The bird hunkered off—with the other two jostling and nudging it greedily. Jane smacked her hands clean.

We were face to face, and her eyes kept shifting. My stomach clenched when she started to speak. Would she say something awful?

"You have come again, praise God."

"*Praise God.*" Okay. I let my breath out.

"So," I started, "does that mean we can be friends again?" Or did that sound too simple? "I'll try to forget the things you called me," I started again, "if you'll just believe that I didn't mean—that I would never hurt you—"

"Wait." She held a hand up. "I have one behest."

"Behest?"

"Something to ask of you."

I looked up at the gloomy sky—the dark clouds moving, being driven. Then, "Okay." I met Jane's brown eyes. "Ask away," I said.

"Show me proof. Pray, show me proof that you be an angel."

"I…" *How could…?* "But I'm *not*. I told you I come from… another time and place."

One long black panel of her headdress lifted in the rising wind. "Nay. Not your tales and amusements."

"But they're *true*. It's a place in the future, like I said. How can I *show* you?"

She threw her hands up. "I know—I *sense*, I mean"—her eyes held mine—"that you *cannot* be the Devil's emissary." She searched my face. "Yet you have to be from one realm or…"

I think she bit her tongue instead of insulting me again with "or the other."

"Wherefore, I ask and ask myself, would God's own angel give me counsel to forsake Him? Mayhap you meant to test me? Or to speak of the forgiving nature of His love, and I misunderstood you?" She said it again, almost a whisper. "*Have I* misunderstood you? Can you not see why I must speak so boldly as to ask for proof—"

"If I could only prove the *truth*," I said. Then something

came to me. Just something small. But maybe. "Hey." I started digging through my pockets. A Bic pen cap, a puff of lint…

A toonie.

I dusted it off. "Here, look," I said. "This comes from *my* time."

She took it, hesitant at first, cupping both hands around it so it wouldn't blow away. Then she turned it over from queen to polar bear and back again.

"Be this Metal of India?" She tapped the middle part.

"Do you mean gold? Uh-uh. It's just a small amount of money. It's called a toonie."

"Too-nie."

She kept staring at it, then at me. Each time her eyes met mine, she looked a bit less doubtful.

"The year of our Lord, Jane, *two thousand and twelve*?"

I nodded. "Two thousand and twelve, yeah."

"That be—"

I'd done the math a while ago: "It's 460 years from now."

She kept shaking her head. "What might the world be…?"

"Different," I said. "Really different. I've got so much I can tell you."

"Wait." She looked alarmed all of a sudden. "Be it a God-less world?"

"No," I said. "It's just that…What I meant then is just that people…" *How to reassure her?* "We use different names. We talk about God differently."

There was silence for a minute. Just the wind, and a "*Cor-ronk!*" from one of the ravens.

Did I lose her? Did I blow it?

No.

She'd gone back to studying the toonie.

"Jane, pray tell"—I could see her frowning at the modern lettering—"Can-a-da?"

"That's where I live. It's in the New World."

"Nay! You look not at all like a Red Indian."

"There's lots of other people there by now. We kind of... pushed the first ones over."

She dropped her eyes back to the toonie. "Your queen is called Elizabeth?"

"Yeah."

"It sayeth here Elizabeth II."

Did *it? Oh.*

"Who was Elizabeth I, pray tell?"

I took a breath. This felt like risky territory. "Well, it was your cousin."

"But my cousin *Mary* be Queen. Do you mean to tell me she will..."

"Die." I nodded. "In about five years. And then Elizabeth will be queen for forty-five years. Until 1603." Thanks to Mr. Gregor, the date was fresh in my mind.

The tail of Jane's headdress flipped right up now, hiding part of her face. But I could catch enough of her expression to know I was convincing her. And that she was impressed. Even more, it seemed, than when I was "an angel."

"Elizabeth," she whispered, leaning close. "Will she bring the New Faith back?"

"Yes, she will," I said. "She did."

Her face broke into an amazing smile, then she dropped to her knees and started praying—sort of swaying back and forth and mumbling joyfully.

I looked everywhere except at her. All three ravens were still hanging around at the edge of things. I somehow sensed that one of them was Odin. I thought of words like "exultation," and "hallelujah." I thought of a board game, not chess, but a newer one: Jenga. Our connection was like the tower in that game. I was the one who knew both centuries—well, more than *she* could. So it was up to me to say the right things, not the wrong ones, and to overlook things—pull out the stuff we'd never really get about each other, and not send the whole thing crashing.

A colder gust came up as Jane was getting to her feet a minute later. "Mistress Tilney has a fire set in the grate." She dipped her chin into her thick fur collar as she eyed my jeans and sweater. "Do you not feel the cold," she asked, "in…my world?"

"No. Just for the first few minutes."

She pressed the toonie back into my hand. "Lest one of the ravens might be drawn to its shine." What she was really thinking, I suspected, was so no one would find it and accuse her of witchcraft on top of treason—like the unfortunate Anne Boleyn. I slipped it back into my pocket.

"I knew it," she said as we headed for the jailer's house. "I knew in my heart that you could not be evil, just misguided." She said this just as I was saying, "I'm so glad I came back." We tried again and the same thing happened: "All I know is I'm here to be your friend."/"I had no way to call you back to me."

"I know. And I know how hard it is when you can't trust anyone," I said. "Not even your own parents."

She blinked. "'Tis true for you as well?"

"Well, not like yours. But my mother—sometimes she drinks too much." First time I'd ever said it.

Jane nodded sympathetically. "Has she been made to wear the drunkard's cloak? How humiliating for you."

"Drunkard's cloak?"

"The barrel? Back in Bradgate, Ned the blacksmith had to waddle about in one for days. After he pissed in the water trough," she said matter-of-factly, "mistaking it for a latrine."

I laughed. "It hasn't come to that yet. Thankfully."

I rubbed my thumb over the toonie in my pocket. Not enough to buy a drunken mom a drink. Not even bus fare. But it was enough to help Jane believe me. I thought of my feather. Odin and his friends were picking their way around the curve of the next tower, hunched against the weather like old women in black kerchiefs, or…"Hey," I said as we rounded the curve behind them. "The three witches from *Macbeth*." I pointed. "*That's* who they remind me of."

"Of who?"

"Of Shakespeare's witches."

"Who?"

"The playwright?" But she shook her head.

Wasn't *he* even born yet?

The jailer's house came into sight, a plume of smoke rising and twisting from its chimney.

"People from your time and place…" Jane started. She said the words very precisely, still getting used to them as something real, but her eyes, on mine, were curious and trusting. "Do they *do* this? Do they…travel oft?"

"Not oft." I thought of my weird conversation with Megan.

"Or if they do, they sure don't talk about it. People *have* gone to the moon—"

"Away! You truly are a jester." Then she paused a minute. "Namesake?"

Her tone was so different, I steeled myself for what she might say next.

"Since you come from the future, can you tell me what becomes of me?"

15 Galliard (*noun*: type of lively, high-spirited dance)

There are only six layouts to Hydrostone houses. I tell you this in case you should ever be snooping around on the top floor of one to return a yellow notebook—a mission I found myself on the next week. They were built right after the Halifax Explosion, these houses—after the wooden ones that used to stand in this area blew apart. It was a plan right out of *Three Little Pigs*: use building materials that can keep you safe from anything—well, anything on the *outside*.

And for all I know they can.

I was poised between three bedroom doors—all closed—when the doorbell rang. And then a burst of chatter. Crisco had arrived. "What's for grub? I had to *work*, you know." (*We know, already.*) "Cool place, Simon. Cool recliner. Anyone got dibs? It's mine. Hey, Meg. Hey, Tom. Where's Jane?"

She's in the bathroom, someone with a smaller voice likely answered, though really I was standing frozen on the spot. At least the Wongs hadn't made the attic into *another* bedroom, like Meg's parents had done for her. *Meg, return your own evidence next time. Even if he is "so totally and constantly tuned in" to your every move, now that the two of you are an item.*

Secretly, though, I was glad she'd asked me—and not Crisco—to sneak Simon's notebook back.

Take a breath and knock. If someone answers, say I'm looking for the bathroom. Like I don't know where to find it in a Hydrostone the same as Meg's. Like the door isn't half open. Pink bath mat peeking, fluffily. Close it. There.

Door Number One: Generic Teenage Boy.

Door Number Two: The Same.

I stepped into the tidier one—where the green plaid bedspread was more or less on the bed—and looked around at rollerblades lazing on their sides, a desk with a mega-tangle of cords, pine bookshelf. *That* might help. A honk of Crisco-laughter floated up as I stepped gingerly over a puddle of sports socks and bent to read the titles. *Zen and the Art of Motorcycle Maintenance. Maus: A Survivor's Tale.* Simon or his older brother? Hard to say.

I checked the bookshelf in the other room, stepping over a larger puddle of sports socks and etcetera (I didn't look real close). *Zen and the Art of Motorcycle Maintenance. Maus* again. Would someone help me? *Howl and Other Poems. The Collected Works of Edgar Allan Poe.* Hooray.

I took the notebook from my backpack and slipped it beneath a pile of papers on Simon's desk, where eventually he'd find it. This way, he'd never know why Megan had suddenly started giving him the eye. He could choose his own time to "come out," as Megan put it, as her poet. "*Très plus romantique.*"

Downstairs, things had gone quiet. I leaned over the railing and looked at them. Heads bent over papers. Peer editing away. Tom had his back to me, with (one) pen stuck behind his ear. Megan was cross-legged on the couch with her skirt spilling down in lacy scallops, and Simon was sitting on the floor in front of her, one shoulder grazing her knee. Crisco, nearly horizontal in the recliner, caught my eye and flashed me a smile that I had to admit looked pretty real. Hard to believe they'd once seemed so intimidating.

Then I walked into the room.

"Lady Jane has returned," Tom said as I was slinging off my backpack, "with that big sack of books she even takes with her to the can."

I felt my cheeks go red. "Look, will you let it go?" My voice came out too sharp—way too much feeling. "That's the trouble with you," I blundered on. "You never let anything drop."

His cheeks were turning pinkish too. "The trouble with you, kid—you're not quite as sweet as you seem."

"Whoa!" Meg cut in. "Will you stop picking on my—"

"I'm not picking on your friend."

"Would you both not talk about me like I wasn't here?"

Another voice rang out, from the depths of the recliner. "This isn't the War of the Roses," it said. Crisco pressed some button and it zoomed her up. Chipped eggplant fingernails on the leatherette arms, followed by the rest of her. "Come on, you guys." Her kohl-rimmed eyes were a faded-denim blue I'd never really noticed. Right now, they moved back and forth between Tom and me.

She got up and pulled him off his chair. She actually took his hand, and mine, and tried to bring the two of us together. Tom was letting her. His cheeks were still a bit flushed. Such light skin—nearly delicate—on a guy with dark hair and eyes. Dark eyes with golden flecks; *you could fall right in.*

"Don't fight," Crisco said. "You guys'd look so cute." And I yanked my hand away—suddenly way too self-conscious. What a comedown for Tom—hot for Megan, and then to be told he'd look "cute" with someone he thought of as "kid." She sure had a way of saying the wrong thing.

Simon broke the silence that set in then. "Have a seat, Jane." He jabbed a thumb at the spot beside Megan, then tugged on his springy hair. "I'm getting sick of Thomas Cromwell. Think I'll tell Gregor I'm gonna change my subject. Do one of the ravens."

"Cool." Crisco scrolled a finger through the air. "You could describe what's happening in the Tower, looking down."

"Except they can't fly high enough to look down," I said.

Meg said, "I thought they just couldn't get over the walls."

"No, they can only go about so high." I held a hand up.

"We could ask Alexa," Tom put in, "since she's actually been there." And I think my eyes popped—from holding in a sudden urge to scream. I looked at the coffee table, where someone's draft was waiting to be edited. It was Tom's. *Revenge? Here's hoping.* I reached for my red pen.

Even the nursery rhymes that come from the Tudor period are violent. Take "Mary, Mary, Quite Contrary." (Queen) Mary grows "silver bells, cockle shells, and pretty maids all in a row." But "cockle shells" was a nickname for thumbscrews, and "pretty maid" another word for the guillotine. Also, the severed heads of criminals and traitors were displayed on tall poles at the entrance to London Bridge—and left there to rot.

People clung to religion (and magic and astrology). Catholics and Protestants said each other would be barred from heaven. But people often switched faiths if it would save their lives—or make them richer. In a Tudor court, a thirst for wealth and power ran deeper than either loyalty or faith.

This was a draft?

Sir Thomas More wasn't perfect. But at least he believed in something more noble than raw ambition. He stayed true to his faith even though it cost him his head. In this, he stands out from all the others.

No way! I pulled my pen cap off:

Lady Jane Grey did the same thing!

My head filled up with pictures of the life she probably *could* have had, otherwise—a life in "great rooms" and libraries, and riding well-groomed horses over what she called "the heath." Ditching that sucky Guildford down the road somehow. If I could only make her see—but, *"you must vow that you will speak of it no more."* That's what she had insisted, warming her hands over the fire, the day we made up from our fight.

I tried not to think about her question on the Green that day—hardest question I had ever been asked. I had looked her up already—that's what I told her—and we knew nothing about her in my time; she apparently hadn't been major enough to go down in history. *"But you knew from the start that I was Jane Grey"*—and I said that was because I'd heard her ladies talking. She looked so sad. Guessing I was lying—and guessing why? I hoped not. What she said was, *"'Tis a shame to be forgotten."*

Meg nudged me. "Jane, you look so…stricken. Surely Tom's writing isn't *that* bad?"

"What?" It took me a second to snap back.

The rest of them were laughing. Not at me—at some drawings Crisco was passing around. Meg grabbed one and we looked at it together. It was Mr. Gregor, dressed up like Henry VIII. In color pencil. She was brilliant, I had to admit.

"Doesn't he look chi-chi in his waistcoat?" Her smile was almost shy.

"In his doublet," I said. "Yeah. Does he ever."

"And his purple stockings."

"Hose." I was going to the Tower every day now—sometimes before school and again at night—picking up a lot.

Meg looked at me. "You know your stuff," she said. And I kept going. "These"—I pointed to the hose on Mr. Gregor's lower legs—"have the coolest name. Nether stocks." Then I looked Crisco full in the face. "I wish I could do something this awesome."

We all laughed at a new sheet she was holding up: Mr. Gregor back in his regular clothes, but leaping through the air in a Renaissance dance step. He was brandishing a blackboard eraser, his thin hair lifting, under a cloud of chalk dust like a halo.

"King Gregor, practicing the Julliard."

"Galliard. Sorry."

Tom caught my eye. "But I bet you can't *dance* it."

What was *with* him?

"Well"—I'd show him, I figured—"Actually. As a matter of fact."

I got up. I jumped onto one foot and brought the other one halfway up my shin, then jumped again and reversed my feet in one quick motion. My anger at Tom wiped out the fact that this was totally not something I'd do.

Someone clapped, and Simon pushed the coffee table further out of the way.

"Uh-uh." I backed off. "That's it, guys."

But Meg said, "Oh, come on. I'll do it with you."

So, one foot forward, one foot back—I showed Meg, just like Jane had shown me that very morning. She'd been shocked when I said I didn't know the Galliard. "*Then how can you go to your masques and promenades?*"

I held my back straight and my chin at a haughty angle. I would have made my lady proud.

Forward one-two-three, back one-two-three, *leap*. On my way up I could nearly see her—brocaded sleeves fanned out, arms lifting in encouragement. And as I came down it was them I saw, and bits of wall and window blind, and with each jump—*faster, faster*—the distance between her and them, and then and now, seemed to fade a bit, to collapse. Meg, familiar, her own blur of motion. Simon's red-tipped hair. Crisco clapping out a rhythm. Tom. *Tom. Tom.* His thumbs hooked through his belt loops. His dark eyes.

The wind was scattering leaves across the sidewalk. I kicked and shuffled through them, walking home. No one looking. Or…I glanced over my shoulder. *Tom?* Too far away to tell. But no, he wouldn't be coming in this direction.

"We could ask Alexa. Since she's actually been there."

I kicked a bunch of leaves a little harder.

Someone had a woodstove going, and I stopped and breathed it in. The day before, the Partridges had burned a huge log in the hearth downstairs. The heat met us at the door when we came in from the Green—and the roar. Part beast, part...vacuum. A fire burning at full throttle—how it can mesmerize you, suck you in.

Burning wood and dry leaves crunching. My dad flickered through my mind. Camping trips, hiking. Sometimes I'd go with him, or a bunch of us: my mom, and my Aunt Peggy and her partner, Kate. Other times, he just loved to take off and...*no.* "Let that thought go." That's how Mom's Buddhist ex-boyfriend would have put it. Let it fly away. Up the side of Needham Hill.

The hill that divides the Hydrostone from the newer streets and the harbor was a lumpy silhouette tonight. The prickly outlines of some evergreens along its side were soldiers, crouched and stealthy. A war party of Iroquois sneaking up on a Huron village? Or—I thought of Traci's deep-voiced cousin (who Meg and I both used to crush on), in Afghanistan right now. But mostly I thought of Mary's knights and foot soldiers when they marched on London to claim her rightful crown.

This night—this one right here—was weird. And weirder. Time pushing in and out like an accordion, and now the wind— it seemed to be calling my name. Or hers? Who was it after? I glanced around, and there was no one but the Tom-not-Tom guy. He raised a hand. It looked like it *might be* Tom, so I waved back but kept going. No way would he be following me—a girl not as sweet as she seemed. A Megan's sidekick of a girl. One who gave Renaissance dance demonstrations (*god, what was I thinking?*).

Stairs Place. My street. I turned the corner and cut across the boulevard. The wind had at least stopped calling, but jack-'o-lanterns were grinning from some of the windows. Each of them had a fire lighting up its mouth and eyes.

16 Dormouse (*noun*: someone sleeping, dozing, slumbering)

The cold eye sweeping back and forth across the library lawn is not of human substance, but is tied to human purpose. That's what the razor-sharp beak might say if it would speak in any of the human tongues. If it would deign to do so. Circling through time together. Bound by myth, and by a taste for all that glitters.

A girl with a dark green backpack is just going into the library. Me.

Me on replay...

Thinking it is just another day. Except the bird knows better. Straining, he pumps his wings and lurches to the low, stone wall—the highest point he can get to. Watching the pigeons who strut, who look down from the roof of the library, taking flight for granted. Watching the people on the benches by the chip truck, French fries wagging, tantalizing, from their fingers. Waiting until the girl comes back out.

That's why this dream's so freaky: I see myself through his eyes—

See me walk across the grass to Megan. "Toc-toc-toc!" His call is fast and loud. Some people turn. They point. But she, she/I, walks on, oblivious. Her backpack full, she looks as hunched as he does. Leaning forward from the weight.

17   Writ (*noun:* document, missive, letter)

My mother was home so much the next couple of weeks, I was starting to think she was being dumped.

"Where's Dave these days?" I tried to keep my tone light. *How many times had he been here since that dinner party—the one he wasn't at?*

"He's run off his feet with clients." She kept sorting through a pile of student essays. "Lots of weddings to shoot."

In November? Meet Analise Grey, Queen of Denial.

I was in the doorway of her study, where posters of gallery openings overlapped on the burgundy walls, and a strip of small gray-trimmed windows looked onto our postage-stamp backyard and then the lane. A thick sheet of glass stretched from the top of one two-drawer filing cabinet to another—my mom's very cool homemade desk. One wall was floor-to-ceiling art books, plus a few English literature books she'd brought home from my dad's office at Dalhousie University, like his enormous *Riverside Shakespeare*, which I was heading for now.

"Working on your English project?" Her smile was bright, approving.

"History."

"Jane. Don't put all your energy into the one subject where you're already doing—"

I flinched. "I'm doing fine in everything."

And if she only knew I, too, was teaching—Lady Jane having gone for my offer to tutor her, after all. Our curriculum included English in My Time and Place.

"Hey there," Jane had said when I arrived this morning, and I'd said, "Hey, my lady. How's it going?"

"Going good," she answered carefully. "I like your tunic. It's"—she stopped to think a minute—"cool. It's passing well-suited with your britches."

"Uh-huh." I paused. "You're doing great. Here's a new word." I patted my hunter green top and spun around to provide a full view. "It's called a hoodie."

"Who-dee. That will be due to the head covering, forsooth."

I propped the *Riverside* on the edge of Mom's desk and scanned the introduction. What I wanted to know could be found online, but I liked the feel of the paper, thin as onionskin—and the connection with my dad.

"What are you looking for?"

"When Shakespeare lived."

"Sixteenth century."

"Yeah, but when? Oh, here. Born in 1564," I said. Eleven years after Jane's time.

My mom and I were in Mode Two territory these days,

with the occasional foray into Mode One. Not wanting to let
my guard down, I was moving carefully—sort of like stepping
around Simon's sports socks. Though my mother—leaning
back in her springy-looking ergonomic chair, with one slim
ankle resting on the other blue-jeaned knee—looked way too
classy for that comparison.

"I didn't think you even liked him," she said.

"How would I know? I've hardly read him."

"*What?*" she said, and then a light went on: "I mean *Dave!*"
And we both laughed.

"Dave's okay." *Was* okay is what I nearly said. A big guy
with a camera around his neck like an extra appendage. The
best of them—and he was one, since he was nice to her—kept
things a little more even, made things run more smoothly.
Then, one drunken outburst or two, and they'd split.

The landline rang. She tensed and rushed to the kitchen.

Then, "Jane," she called, "it's Traci." Her voice was flat.

Have a heart, I always wanted to tell those guys. *She's sick.
It isn't her fault.* But I figured I'd take off too if I had someplace to go. Like a grandparent who was still alive and lived
anywhere near us, or an aunt except for Peggy, who we didn't
speak to anymore.

Mom left the kitchen, her shoulders slumped in a way I'd
never noticed until now. *Just her and me.* I felt as guilty for my
thoughts as if I'd said them out loud. I held my hand over the
receiver while Traci was talking. *I won't leave you,* I mouthed
into the air. *I won't tell anyone your secret.*

"You there, Jane?"

"Sorry—yeah."

"I tried your cell, but it was off."

Oh, right—from earlier, so it wouldn't ring and yank me back to the present. I'd forgotten to turn it back on.

"How did it go with Simon's notebook?" Traci asked.

"It went fine. Think I'll add courier to my resume," I said, "for Career and Life Management class. Can do undercover jobs."

I didn't know then where my next job would take me.

One day when I arrived, Jane had a box open on the bed beside her.

"Namesake!" She gave a start, but I was so busy gawking I hardly noticed.

"What *is* that?"

It was her writing box, she said. Did I not have one like it? I shook my head. "No way."

It was amazing—intricate, like a lot of things in her time. Like the prayer book, for one. Clouds floated across the powder blue inside of the box's lid, and pink-cheeked women floated too, trailing scarves behind them—every detail beautifully filled in.

"Could I...could I take a look?"

She seemed hesitant at first. But then she nodded, with a little smile—my enthusiasm winning her over. She opened three small drawers in the front and showed me lumps of wax in two of them. From the third drawer, she brought out a metal ring—a sealing ring, she called it—engraved with her initials (ours). The letters were backwards, of course, to be pressed into melted wax. Even so, and with all their swirlyness, I could make out *JG*.

You didn't get a new one for your married name? I nearly asked. Then I remembered how far she'd been demoted. This sealing ring and writing box, and even the brown silk dress she was wearing and the headdress with the bright gold stitching, the one that made her eyes shine—this all came from the world where she *used to* belong.

"See this." She tipped the writing box to one side and another drawer slid out—a long thin one that ran along the back like a secret passage.

"Neat!"

"'Tis where my quills go. See?"

Quills? I picked one up. It was a stiff gray feather. Softer than Odin's. "What kind of bird?"

"A goose."

"Hey"—I smiled—"is that where Mother Goose got her name?" But Jane frowned. It looked like Mother Goose wasn't born yet either.

The only thing left was a shallow tray. Jane pulled it partway open to show me the inkwell tucked underneath. And that's when my hand shot out, as if on automatic pilot. "Hey!" I took the letter that was tucked into the far corner.

A letter *to* Jane? No, it was *from* her. JG was pressed into the pool of dark red wax. The handwriting was delicate and tiny, nearly covering the square of parchment.

"How can you write so small—"

Then I looked up and saw the hurt in her eyes.

"Oh, sorry! Here." I held the letter out; Jane reached for it. And in the space between her thumb and mine on the cream-colored parchment, the name it was addressed to suddenly jumped out. The first letter was an *E* with its

bottom line curling up—like an *F* on skis. An *E* for Edward.
Seymour.

Now I got it. Now I knew why she'd seemed hesitant.

"A married woman. I know full well how it must appear."
She ran her hands along the folds of her skirts. "I felt a need
to have him see, in mine own hand"—she took a breath and
looked right at me—"that I would never have broken our
promise had I not been beaten black and blue."

"I'm on your side. I'm not judging you."

"Nay? Verily?"

"I'd never. But how will you get it to him?"

"Alas, *no* way. A letter from a queen disgraced, a prisoner
in the Tower. Who would carry such a tainted missive—"

"Oh!" I said. "Don't call it that."

"And wherefore not?" She gave a laugh, her edgy one.
"'Tis true. Imagine me saying to Mistress Tilney, 'Shall we
hire a messenger?' And pay him with what? There be a scullery maid"—she dipped her chin to indicate the Partridges'
kitchen below us—"who be taking leave this day to visit family
in Smithfield. Shall I run behind her: 'Will you take a detour
to dispatch my letter?' I thinketh not."

"How long would it take her?"

"'Tis not the *point*. My point be just to say—"

"How long?" I asked again.

Outside, ravens called to one another on the Green. Jane
turned her head toward the window.

"How long? And in which direction?"

I could hear the distant strains of someone playing a
stringed instrument.

"The Seymours' city house be on the Southwark side.

Two hours on foot." She shrugged. "Faster, mayhap, on a skiff across the Thames." Her voice was offhand, nearly casual. But it was casual on purpose. When she turned and looked full at me, her very freckles seemed to be radiating: *Would you?*

Sure, I would. You could even say I have experience.

18 Wench (*noun*: girl, lass)

The trouble started with a dog.

I had flattened myself against the weathered shingles of a house to keep from getting walloped for the umpteenth time—this time by a man with a tray of bloody-looking sausages, hollering, "Sheep's feet, 'ot puddins! Sheep's feet, 'ot puddins!"

Then I nearly got soaked by someone emptying a chamber pot. I jumped back just in time—and heard an upstairs window slam shut.

London.

Bad place to be invisible.

I stepped out then and nearly collided with the dog. But *she* didn't plough into me as if I wasn't there. She looked up and fixed her wet black eyes on mine.

What was going on? I think my heart stopped.

She was giving my legs a thorough sniffing.

I saw the little boy then. Blue hat, white feather. "Papa! Papa, look!"

The man in tall boots behind him.

People funneled past on either side.

Had I suddenly turned visible?

The boy was pointing. "Look at Ollie! She be sniffin' at a ghost or som'at. She be sniffin' at the air!"

And then it clicked. She was an *animal*. Like Odin. Odin had seen me from the start.

My knees buckled in relief. I leaned down to scratch the dog's wiry chin, and her stumpy tail wagged even faster. The boy erupted in a fit of giggles.

"No, no. You can't have *that*." I held Jane's letter behind my back in one hand, out of reach of Ollie's long pink tongue. It felt good to be seen—and to have my other hand licked thoroughly.

I hadn't realized how scary this would be—to be in this wild, chaotic place without even Jane to see me. I'd followed the Partridges' scullery maid through the gates at Middle Tower, and watched her hobnail boots make patterns in the dust as she headed to Smithfield. And I'd come, alone, to London.

Did I hear something first? Was there talk, I wondered afterward, *and pointing*? Or just the quick hand reaching out for what I *did* notice.

Yank.

The letter. Pulled from between my unsuspecting thumb and finger.

Stupid—to have held it out like that. I got that then—even in my panic. The letter could be seen. It wasn't part of me. It was part of *here*.

I spun around. Caught a glimpse of something—a square of whitish paper in a hand. A bare hand, across the narrow street. I pushed my way toward it, through a press of people, nearly getting run down by a wagon full of barrels—full of *fish*. I pinched my nose. And yes, there it *was*. I could see through a gap that formed behind the wagon. It was the letter, in a hand that was moving way faster than *I* could make it through the crowd. A tuft of blonde hair, swinging. Tail end of a braid? A girl's hand? A girl, yes. In a whole gang of kids. Then—

Gone.

I looked around for a place they might have ducked into. Most of the houses here had stores at their ground level, with wooden shutters drawn back to open them to the street. Signs swung above, on chains, from where the top floors of the houses jutted out: a fish-shaped skeleton, a grimacing fish with a hook through its mouth. *Where would a gang of kids get to?*

"Twelve-pence-a-peck oysters!" someone chanted, and "Catch o' the day!" A cat darted from an alleyway, and a rock landed just behind it. I heard a girl's voice: "Bloody brute!"

I stepped closer. More voices. Kids' voices. I slipped into the alley and made my way to a dingy courtyard just behind.

A tall boy was in the middle of a throng of kids, wiping his mouth with the back of one hand. "Dratted mog was about to eat me dinner, if it be your business." He glowered at a girl who had a scrawny build like his. "It had me name on it." Then he snapped his fingers. "What would it *be*, sis? Give it over." They had the same straw-colored hair, his with a cowlick and hers in ratty braids.

She, too, was taller than the other kids, and when she held Lady Jane's letter up, none of their outstretched hands could reach it. "Said I wanted to shew you, is all," she told her brother, while the other kids crowded in, the smaller ones on tiptoe.

"A seal," said one. "Och! Like a gentleman's."

I reached over one boy's lice-infested head (I could actually see them streaming across his part) and tried to snatch the letter from the girl's hand. Her mouth fell open and her light brown eyes widened. She was young. No more than eight or nine. But her grip was so firm I knew I couldn't get the letter without ripping it.

I let go and she fell back a step and shook her head, staring at her hand. Then she snapped back to her reality.

"What do you reckon?" asked a bow-legged boy whose hair was limp and patchy. "Do you take it for a nobleman's?"

"Methinks"—she clutched the letter to her chest—"that it belongs to no one but the queen herself. I plans to take it to her, to the Tower of London."

"Good luck," scoffed her brother. "The queen be gone to Whitehall."

"Well, to Whitehall then."

"'Tis just the young one at the Tower. That young Jane. The one whose head be fixed for choppin'."

"*Her*," the girl said. "Yea. We seen her sailing down the Thames and no one even *knew* her." She pulled her shawl tight, still clutching Jane's letter. Her shawl was full of holes and she wore shoes she might have made herself: coarse black twine, looped like Roman sandals around the baggy brown feet of her hose. "The queen," she said, "the true queen. She will smile upon me when I bring her letter. 'I needs a daughter just like you to bring my ale, and to mend my garter,' 'tis what she will say."

"Daft is what *I* say," said her brother. The others laughed and she turned her head to glare at them.

The kid with the patchy hair spoke up again. "We ought to take it to someone who can read."

"And did anyone ask for your tuppence worth?" The tall boy curled his lip; he had a cruel-looking mouth. "Give it over."

"Nay! 'Tis mine. I found it."

"Where?"

Her mouth flew open. Then she stopped and took a breath. "'Twas in the air."

There was silence for a full beat. "Say again?"

"'Twas in the air. 'Twas...rather...floating."

He raked his fingers through his cowlick. "Daft! You be the daftest wench in all of Christendom!"

She kicked him in the shin. It must have hurt her, through her makeshift shoe. She bit down as if to keep from howling.

He laughed, and she moved in close again. From where I was standing at the edge of the group, I could see her mouth working before she thrust her chin up. Her brother cursed when the spit landed on his collar, and a gasp ran through the crowd. "Your life will be worth piss!" He cocked a finger at the tip of her braid—the last part of her to whip out of sight around the nearest corner.

We all ran to catch her. Me first. But I got trampled, and someone came down hard on my foot.

I lost them. I ended up alone—alone and limping down a street I hadn't seen before. It was packed with people, but she wasn't one of them. None of them were here.

What would happen? Who would get hold of the letter, and what would this do to Jane? What would it do to her Edward Seymour?

A man in a scarlet cape rode past, the feather in his cap nearly brushing the sign above him as it creaked on its chains. Would the girl try to stop a man like him? He'd ride right past her—for all I knew he'd gladly ride right *over* her—but would he stop if she waved the letter? Would she ask him to read it?

My foot felt better now, but it hardly mattered. *Which way to go?* The stuff in the storefronts seemed to be mocking me—me and my useless attempts to help Jane. A birdcage, like a room to trap a lady in. A display of pewter mugs that reminded me of the Tower guard spitting into the moat that night—disgusting. Higher up: dead rabbits hanging—*worse*. These made me think of Crisco and her announcement of the week: she was turning vegan now. And of Megan looking at her with a gleam of admiration.

I leaned into one of the storefronts for a second and nearly got stepped on again, this time by a man in dark robes. "G'day barrister," the shop woman said. And when he reached to tip his hat in reply, his fur cuff grazed my cheek. Prickly.

This was a jumble of a shop—scarves, gloves, two-pronged forks, mousetraps (big—or were they rat traps?), writing boxes (not as nice as Jane's) and, propped at an angle, a row of mirrors in wooden frames. The glass was clear, like mirrors now. But the barrister's multiple faces peering up from the counter were a bit longer-nosed than his already long-nosed face beside me.

And me, I was nobody. Capital *N*. There was nothing in the mirrors where I should have been. Just framed pieces of the street behind me. A gleaming sash. A fringe of shawl. A horse going by, flash of boot in the stirrup. The midsection of a woman in a stained white apron, with a tray of something strapped around her. A thin arm reaching, a straw-colored braid—

I whipped around.

Yes, it was *her*.

She was on the run again, Jane's letter in one hand and a stolen pastry in the other, leaving the woman shouting, "Hooligan!" and "Stop, thief!" No one chased her, though. Just me.

I lost her once and had to double back. She'd slipped into another alley and around a bend. I caught sight of her, finally, thankfully, across a scrubby patch that looked like some kind of brickyard; she was perched on a crooked back stoop. I slowed down, panting and huffing.

There was the letter—on the step beside her.

Getting close, I noticed how intensely she was munching her pastry, closing her eyes to concentrate on every bite.

When she started talking, those toffee-colored eyes looked faraway and dreamy.

"It be a blessing it fell into loyal hands"—she held them out—"like these. Nay, no one will miss me at home, Your Grace. 'Tis just me brother and me da and me. Me mam went down in the Black Death. And me brother be an idjut, if the truth be told. May not even notice I be gone."

She swallowed her last bite and was licking her fingers when I reached for the letter.

"Thank you kindly," she was saying. "I would *love* a spot of ale to wash me fritter down."

I didn't look back. I didn't want to see her face when she realized the letter was gone.

I came out in an unfamiliar street. The letter was safely tucked into my back pocket—and hidden by my hoodie—but I was stressed out about time. Something might wake me up pretty soon and send me home, and I hadn't even found the bridge. My view was blocked by all the houses. This was another crowded street, and as I walked in the direction that led to the river—or so I was hoping—it swelled with people even more.

Dirty London. Violent. You could sort of say Mr. Gregor had warned me. The air was a mix of smells, including people smells like pee and stale sweat. And fights were breaking out— I dodged some jabbing elbows as I wove my way past one.

Mr. Gregor had also talked about those heads at the entrance to the bridge, the ones Tom had mentioned in his draft. Birds would circle—black scavenger birds called kites—and they'd peck the eyes out. Note to self, marked *High Priority*: When you get there, if you *do* get there, Do Not Look Up.

A wagon lumbered along beside me, piled high with bales of hay. The driver sat on his bench, tapping his foot and grumbling. It was like my time, like a traffic jam on Robie Street—except for the reins hanging slack in his leather-gloved hands. We were packed in so tight I could have touched the horse's low-slung belly. The wagon's running board came dangerously close to my head.

The driver spotted someone he knew. "Be that Sam?" he called. Or Joe. I wasn't paying much attention. But they must have asked him where he was going, and my ears perked up at his answer:

"To the tattingworks. Over to the Southwark side."

The famous bridge: It was a street, a shopping mall, a neighborhood stretched across the Thames. It was great to be sitting up and taking things in again (I had kept my eyes trained down until I sensed that we were over the water—and safely past the heads). The houses that lined both sides of the bridge were five and six stories tall, a lot of them with storefronts at the bottom. From my vantage point on top of the hay, I caught all the action: a juggler tossing apples, a skinny-tailed monkey hunched on someone's shoulder. Things felt even more intense here than on the city streets because of the arched stone ceiling that blocked out the sky. It made me dizzy to look up that far; I gripped the twine that held the bales in place.

"A ring for your finger!" someone shouted from a stall.

"What do ye lack? What do ye lack?"

Then we were out again, on a stretch of bridge that was open to the sky and water. No roof. No houses. I looked down—I mean *way* down—to the Thames. There was nothing to keep us from plunging into it except a low stone wall, about as tall as a guardrail on a highway. The river rushed and gathered into rapids around the stone supports that stuck out just above water level. I watched the blue-black water crash against them, sending up spumes of white foam.

Then I pulled Jane's letter from my pocket and gently bent it the other way, against the curve my butt had made in it. No need to hide it way up here. With my thumbnail, I wiped away a sticky spot—a bit of "fritter."

Some cows came toward us, bumping one another with their big-boned hips, and an oncoming wagon got jostled toward our side of the road and nearly hit us. My driver inched away, neat as clockwork, jerking the reins. I felt safe with him despite the Thames below us. Things would be different when it was time to get off, though. How would I *get* off, even? Tricky, unless he was going really slow at the time. And if I found the Seymours' house—a big *if*, even with Jane's directions—I'd still have to find Edward. And then what? Drop the letter at his feet?

"Sheer folly, and sheer hope." That's what Jane had said herself about this mission—more objective, likely, than her description of Edward: "Hair of gold and eyes of sparkling blue."

A man headed toward us on a chestnut horse, cupping a hand over his mouth and shouting, "A message for the queen!" Wagons squeezed to either side and people scattered to let him through. His horse was groomed until it shone—or was that sweat?

"A message for the queen! Make way!" A child darted out from somewhere—right in front of us—and we veered toward the water, sharp.

Our wheel must have rammed the guardrail. The load started to lift, like it was breathing out, and the bale I was on went sliding and me with it. I fell flat on my back and hung onto the twine with both hands to keep from getting thrown—hanging on with *both hands*—

And saw the letter fly loose and go where *I'd* nearly gone. Down. Way down. Pulled under the churning blue-black surface of the water.

I closed my eyes to block everything out. The load had shifted back again and settled, and we were on the move. I could feel that—that and a burning in my palms from gripping the twine. I couldn't find a way to save her life. And now I'd messed up the one thing I could have done for her. The one favor.

I stayed like that, eyes closed. Letting the tears come. Flat on my back on the hay. I knew we'd gone into a covered section of the bridge again; I could hear the hawkers. Someone was shouting, over and over, "What ye lack?" Then we were back out in the open and the rhythm changed again. I sensed that we were leaving the bridge. That's when I opened my eyes and—

What...? What was *going on?*

They were staring down at me. At least the ones who still had eyes. There was a greasy, blackish coating on their skin. Their hair was pulled out in chunks. There was an old man, bloated, and a woman with red-painted lips and a terrified face. And more, lots more. On long stick necks. Some had holes in their cheeks, with strips of flesh hanging. This one's mouth was open, like a scream got frozen. "No!" And that one's nose was half torn off. "No! Go away!" One with one eye dangling...

Reaching...for me. "No! Get out!" Arms reaching down and coming around me. *Arms...?* They were...warm. They— "go away!"...

They were my mother's arms. Bits of my room, floating behind her.

Almondy smell of her shampoo.

"Jane! What's wrong? It's okay." She was holding me, and I stopped fighting. I could feel her heartbeat. I clung to her. Clung like I'd never let go.

19 Mew (*verb*: coop up, confine, shut up)

I tipped my mug and swirled the Ovaltine around, breathing in the familiar smell of scalded milk.

"Sure you don't want to tell me about your—?"

"No. I just wanna forget it." I glanced at her quickly. My eyes, like the rest of me, were readjusting to the modern world. A tea towel looped over the fridge-door handle. The microwave on its perch.

"I must have scared you with all that screaming."

"Mrs. Lynde too, likely, through the wall." (The old nickname had stuck in Mom's mind also.) She brushed my bangs back from my forehead; they were clumped with sweat. And when she stepped away her nose was crinkled.

"Something smells like straw, Jane. Weird. I think it's coming off your clothes."

I sniffed my shoulder.

Hay, to be exact. Because I just got back from London Bridge, where I was hitching a ride to some kind of mattress factory—

No, I didn't say it. But my mouth was actually open to say something…*strange is going on.* "Mom?" I started. But she moved and her ruby-colored earring swayed. The splash of red against her skin, where her hair was tucked behind one ear—it nearly set me off again. I shut my eyes. *No, keep them open*. I wrapped my fingers around my mug—it was my Garfield mug—to feel the heat in it coming through.

Mom stared at me from across the table. "What *is* it, Jane?" Her voice was gentle, coaxing.

I thought they'd be on the other *side. That's* when *I closed my eyes. At the* first *side of the bridge.*

My screaming must have really freaked her. Not as freaked as she'd be if she thought I was nuts, though. And, well, she'd smelled the hay—if she thought *she* was losing it too. Talk about drive you to drink.

I wish you were someone I could lean on.

What I really said was, "Nothing. Just that smell. How strange. It's fading." I sniffed again. "Pretty much gone."

It was a dream. The whole thing was just a dream, I tried to tell myself. This room, *this* was real. The copper kettle shining on the flat black surface of the woodstove. My mother, nearly glowing with Mode One energy. My life. Our lives. Her sweater a soft, mossy green.

"That color looks nice on you."

"Oh, thanks." She smoothed it over her hips and flicked at a speck of lint.

I was plugged into the present enough, now, that I could feel her hesitation. "By the way, honey, I still haven't seen you wear that blue sweater."

"There's a party next week," I said. "I'm wearing it to that." And she looked so pleased that I promised myself to get the sweater back from Crisco and make this true. "A bunch of us from History might be going."

She snapped her fingers. "Right. That…Tom. Tom

Kantor? He called."

"Called here?"

"He said he couldn't get you on your cell. Said he wanted to ask you something about homework."

"When?"

"Just after I got in from class," she said. "I told him you were having a nap."

"That's so embarrassing!"

"Embarrassing?"

"Like a daycare kid."

She raised an eyebrow. "Jane. If anything, he sounded kind of nervous."

"He doesn't like me, if that's what you're thinking. He likes Megan."

"Is that right?" She didn't try to deny Megan's charms. Like I've said, my mom's not stupid. But that hopeful-and-maybe-happy-for-you glint didn't fade completely from her hazel eyes. "Things can always change."

"Not this time." I took a sip of Ovaltine.

"You never know. It's one thing to look back at the past." She rested her chin on her thumbs, and brought her pointing fingers together and aimed them at me. "But a much harder thing to see the future."

I groaned. A running joke—Mom's way of making every-day thoughts sound like philosophical statements. The World According to Grey, my dad used to tease her.

"Speaking of Meg," I said. "Guess who she's going out with? Guess who's been writing her poems?"

"Poems! How lovely." She named a boy who lived across the lane. Cute. But about to come out of the closet, I figured.

"Nope. Try again."

She frowned, considering.

"Simon Wong!" I told her, and she shook her head. "Little Simon with his Etch A Sketch."

A while later, I was on my bed with the *Booke of Prayre* open, sifting through the pages, but scared. My eyes drifted up to the poster Mom had given me from *It Might Get Loud*: three guitars just hanging there, attached to nothing—which suddenly creeped me out. A cardigan was draped over my half-open closet door, one dark sleeve poised.

I *would* only land where Jane was? That was one of the rules, right?

We had figured one thing out—and tested it. If I went there more than once the same day, anytime before midnight, it was still the same day in her world too. And I knew she'd be expecting me now, hoping for good news. I'd been setting my clock to call me home—ever since that long night on the ramparts. I set it now, for twenty minutes. Not that the minutes or hours in the two worlds matched up—but it did mean I'd be called back before *too* long.

Would I land there some day in the middle of Jane's execution? That's what was scaring me most.

Not *this* time, though. At least not yet.

I leaned against my pillow and started turning pages. A gold-colored *C*, surrounded by white starbursts in a deep blue sky...A few more pages and I came to it:

Have mercy upon me O God,
according to thy loving-kindness:
according unto the multitude of thy
tender mercies...

And I was back.

When my vision cleared, Jane was hurrying toward me across the Green.

It wasn't very late here yet, the sun just setting. But the cobblers and soap-boilers and whoever they all were seemed to be gone for the day. Gone home to smelly, scary London.

Would they all have seen those heads?

I suppose, at some point.

And Jane. I guess she would have too.

She pulled her cape tighter around her shoulders, crossing the nearly empty Green. "Did you find him, pray tell?" Then my expression must have registered with her. She bit her lower lip as she looked away.

"I'm so sorry," I said.

"Nay." She waved a hand but couldn't meet my eyes yet. "We knew it was sheer folly."

She reached to take her letter.

"My lady..."

Then she looked straight at me—brown eyes glistening— while I explained the whole thing. "The only good news," I said, in the end, "is it's safely in the Thames."

"And you know beyond a doubt no one could fish it out from there?"

I shook my head. "It's toast."

"It—pardon?"

"Yes. I'm absolutely sure. I'm so sorry. Look—if you could write another one I could try again." Did I really *mean* this?

But Jane shook her head.

"'Tis done. I have heard worse tidings in my life." I think she meant this to be comforting. "And I shall again, I daresay."

Then like a joke—a sick joke—we noticed someone bustling toward us across the Green. The light was fading now and it took me a second to recognize her. Plump features on a sallow little pancake of a face. The jailer's wife.

"By your leave, my lady. I have orders to fetch you. To bring you to your chamber."

"Have I a visitor to see me?"

Her eyes dropped. "Nay."

Jane scanned the Green. "Because the night is nigh? I shall be along forthwith," she reassured her. But Mistress Partridge pulled herself up tall. "It distresses me to say, I have my orders from Lieutenant Bridges. You are no longer at liberty to leave your rooms."

"Wherefore not?"

"A message has arrived. A man came riding from the Southwark side, with news"—she took a breath—"with news of Thomas Wyatt. Oh, my lady, he has gathered an army and is marching against the queen."

"A message for the queen. Make way."

Jane gasped. "He must be mad. How large an army?"

"I knowst not. Only that he be proclaiming his intent to bring the New Faith back."

"While bringing doom to me," Jane said.

Unless he succeeded, of course. But if either of them had the slimmest hope of that, it would be treasonous to say so.

"Let us pray for the best." The woman's hands fluttered around, and then landed on Jane's nearest hand and squeezed it. "Let us pray this shall be quelled forthwith, and you shall again be free to—"

"*What?*" Jane pulled away. "To walk again within the ramparts of this Tower?"

She was already heading for the jailer's house. Us with her. "This folly on Tom Wyatt's part will be the death of me."

"No need to think the worst—"

Jane cut her off. "You know as well as I do that my cousin will not spare my life if she has cause—if she has *any* cause—to fear rebellion. She will not deign to see me once again stuck like a puppet on her throne." She finished with a whisper to herself, biting out each word. "The throne I never wanted."

"Begging your pardon. It be not yourself that Thomas Wyatt would be putting there, my lady, but the Princess Elizabeth."

Jane came to a stop. "Verily? Could you not have said so from the start? It striketh fear in me still," she said, "but it be a far sight better. And a lucky circumstance for Bess to be safely away in the country, and not here, as I am—trussed and ready for the pot."

"Who goes there?" It was a man's voice, from across the Green. We turned. "Be that Mistress Partridge? And our lady?"

He came striding toward us. A lantern swung from his hand, splashing light on the now-fading ground and back onto his tall figure. I could see a flapping wing of dark fur trim and the polished boots of a nobleman—also the red and black uniform of a Tower guard.

Jane dipped her head. "Well met, Lieutenant."

He bowed. "My lady."

We huddled together, me scrunched beside Jane. The lantern threw a spooky-looking light up to their faces, but I could see that the lieutenant's eyes, beneath a thicket of gray brows, were kind.

Jane craned her neck. "No need to look so woebegone, John Bridges. I have already been told the news."

I could see him hesitate.

"Pray, is there more?" she asked, and he waited a second longer. "I hate to say these words. Yea, there be further tidings. 'Tis come out now that your father has a hand in it, my lady. He has joined forces with Tom Wyatt. The two of them part company"—he cleared his throat—"on one point."

Jane's voice was strained. "What point, pray tell?"

"Your lord father," he said, "has declared his intent to put you back on the throne."

20 Moody-mad (*adjective*: wild with rage, furiously angry)

"How come we don't have public executions anymore?"

"Yeah. That's what I wanna know."

"They oughta put a guillotine up on the Commons."

It was Ripley and a few other guys at the back. Five minutes past the bell and Mr. Gregor hadn't shown yet.

"And heads on the Macdonald Bridge!" This from a gentle-looking guy who played violin in the all-city orchestra.

"Will you stop—" Stella tried to protest, and so did Yasmeen. But they got drowned out.

"I know!" said Ripley. "They could prop their mouths open, and you could throw your bridge fare in when you drive by."

"Man, you *are* sick."

"Thanks." This set off more laughter and thumping of desks.

Their words ran through me like the water in the Thames—or in Halifax Harbour. Full of shit, they say. Untreated sewage. Even if you can't smell or see it.

"Listen," one of them hissed. "There's this site I went to. When the Americans and—Iraq, I think—when they were cutting each others' heads off—"

"Or like that sucker on that Greyhound bus—"

"Yeah, cool. But this one's live, man. They stop him, right? And make him get out of the jeep and lean over—"

Mr. Gregor, where are *you?*

"Get outta here," said Ripley. "You serious?"

"Yeah, really, dude."

I was gripping the edge of my desk. White knuckles, all in a row.

"What's the site?" said someone.

"Yeah, what's the site?"

And I was on my feet. "Shut up!" I hollered. "These are real people's lives. In case you never thought of that. And deaths." My voice was so loud the whole room seemed to freeze. Steve Ripley's mouth hung open, and they were sitting there, the bunch of them, with their jaws gone slack, eyes shifting.

I bolted. In the doorway I smashed into a wall of beige corduroy.

"Jane? What on earth?"

All teacherly concern, but on the late side. I pushed past him and kept going. In the nearly empty hall I broke into a run.

A few stragglers turned to look, but there was mostly just the beating of my sneaker feet

get me   get me outta here

get me   get me outta here

and another set of feet somewhere behind me. Mr. Gregor? Meg? *Just leave me. Leave me be.* I'd lost it. Lost my cool in front of everyone. Lost control just like my mother. Yelled in class like a nutcase. Smacked into Mr. Gregor as surely as Mom smashed her car into our fence one time. A hole that's never been fixed.

I skidded around a corner. GIRLS. I pushed the door open and slid into the familiar gleam of sinks and tiles. Latching onto the first sink in the row, I caught my stunned expression in the mirror, and Lady Jane's face seemed to float above me, ghostlike—how she turned, as soon as we'd climbed the steep staircase to what was suddenly, more than ever, her prison.

The question she'd never asked before: "Can you not help me?"

And my pathetic answer: "I don't think so, no."

The Wyatt rebellion would fail—and fail quickly. Jane would know that soon. And the harm it did to her would stick.

I tried to focus on my useless face to push *her* face away, and to keep out flashbacks of those heads on London Bridge. They were all mixed up now with visions of my mother staggering through the house that time, up-ending furniture, Timbit streaking upstairs to escape; and images of stupid boys clicking stupid mice in their sweaty palms—or was it "mouses"? Screw Tom Kantor and his editor's pen.

I turned the cold water on and let it spurt. A knocking started at the door. I splashed my face. *Go away.* I reached up to the paper towel dispenser and the angle of my arm, reflected, creeped me out again. The knocking didn't stop. I wet a sheet of paper towel and pressed it to my forehead. Meg? Why didn't she just come in, then? Or, "Mr. Gregor?" I called. "I'm okay. Really."

The door swung open.

And so did my mouth.

"You don't look so hot to me."

Tom.

Tom?

Please don't see me like this.

"This," I said out loud, "is the girls' washroom."

"Yeah. That's what it says on the door." He pushed back a stray wave of hair. "They're a bunch of jerks." He scanned under the stall doors for feet. "Me too," he added. "Off with yer 'ead. About a hundred times too many."

And my heart went out to him. Like usual.

"No one's perfect. Hey, look at me. Would I have ever got so interested in Lady Jane Grey in the first place if she hadn't been killed?" I'd never thought of this before, and it had an awful ring of truth.

"But you're not into blood and guts."

"No. But maybe I go for tragedy instead." I leaned back against the sink now, facing him. "Maybe it's all the same," I said. "Like there's something bloodthirsty or..." I searched for the right word...

"Voyeuristic?"

"Yeah. About being human."

He looked at me a second too long. Not in a bad way.

"Maybe you're beating up on yourself too much, though. Like, why not beat up on Ripley and those guys? Treat me right and I'll even help you."

I laughed. I wasn't sure if he noticed the edge of hysteria. I was still pressing the paper towel against my face.

Then...*treat me right?* Our eyes met for maybe a millisecond before mine slipped away—down to the vintage Uncle Sam Wants You on his T-shirt, beneath a zip-up hoodie, open. Why *did* he chase me in here, anyhow?

"It sucks," he said. "Being human, sometimes. I do get

what you mean." He pointed: "Did you know that's dripping down your arm?"

"What? Oh." A rivulet of water from the paper towel had trickled down to my wrist and was inching toward the crook of my elbow. I went to catch it but Tom got there first—his index finger like a small electrical charge on my skin.

"It's got some good points though."

I dropped the towel into the garbage. "What does?"

"Being human." He put his arms around me. "There's this." His mouth was coming down to meet mine—

"Wait." I pulled back. "I thought—"

"I was into Megan?"

"Yeah."

He didn't look away. "I was. But she and Simon are tight," he said. "So you've got nothing to feel bad about."

"And you've decided to like me instead?"

He sighed. A pulse jumped in his neck. "It's not like that. It started when I walked you home that time."

"But you've hit on Meg since then."

"Well, after all, she—"

"After all, she's gorgeous."

"After all, *she* was nearly hitting on *me*, if you'd let me finish my own sentence. Not exactly the vibe I was getting from you."

I had to smile. "You've got a point."

"Come here." He pulled me in close again, and my head fit perfectly under his chin. I could feel the vibration in his throat when he started to talk. "It was when we walked to your place, like I said. I started to go to Megan's house, like I'd been planning. But instead I ended up walking around the block, and then...walking around the block again." He dipped me back, like something out of *Dancing With the Stars*. "You could say you confused me."

Can pieces fall into place even better than you've ever dreamt them?

"It took me a while to really get it," he said, un-dipping me.

"That's okay. I've always figured you were kind of slow."

Tom's laugh was deep. His hand was warm on the back of my neck, then he lifted my hair and it made me shiver. My eyes closed and all I was aware of was his lips. Everything else had turned to water. Then the door whooshed open. A couple of shrieks rang out. And the sound of feet rushing away.

"Hey, we're making out in the *girls' washroom*."

I rolled my eyes. "That's what it says on the door."

We pulled apart and I peeked out first. "They're gone. Coast clear." I reached my hand back for him to take it. There was just a pink hall pass, dropped on the floor.

Tom sighed with relief when we rounded the corner and there was still no one in sight. "That wouldn't have looked good on my record."

"You're telling me you have a record?"

"Academic record, idiot. Hey?" He looked at me out of the corner of his eye. "You're not, like, planning to tell everyone that I followed you into the can?"

I didn't say a word. Just smiled.

We were approaching Mr. Gregor's room.

"You ready?" Tom asked.

"Much as I'll ever be."

The door was open, and Mr. Gregor had a piece of chalk raised, per usual. He stopped with it poised in midair. "The

voice of sanity has returned. She's been fetched back." Then he
aimed the chalk at Tom and me. "Come take your seats"—he
looked down at our hands—"your separate seats," and a wave
of laughter swept across the room. It felt like everyone was
watching as our fingers opened, reluctantly letting go.

Violin Boy gave me a sheepish smile—same with Ripley,
whose eyes seemed warmer than I'd noticed. I got thumbs-
up from Alexa, Yasmeen, and Meg. Double thumbs-up from
Stella. When I sat down, Crisco swiveled in her chair to face
me. "Way to go!" she whispered. As in, everybody heard.

My cheeks were glowing, I could feel it. Tom-glow. But
there was something else too. Something I had in common,
now, with Lady Jane. "God forgive me for my sin of pride,"
she'd said on one of my first visits. "My moment of pure
pleasure when they all fell to their knees."

21   Hither (*adverb*: here, to this place)

Falling in love, when your friend has finally got it—really got
it—that she's going to die...

I find her sleeping—tossing, turning—in the afternoon.

She wakes up confused, disoriented.

*What she says to me, of all things: "Are you practicing the steps
I taught you?"*

Steps?

*She nods, like this was urgent. "So you and your Tom can go to
your balls and promenades."*

*"Sure," I lie cheerfully. But, "Shew me, pray," she says, and so I
go up on my toes and jump to one side, then the other. I step forward
one-two-three, back one-two-three. And then the ringing starts. My
phone? Did I forget to turn it off?*

She can sense me fading. "Pray, leave me not. Not yet."

Stay with her. One-two-three, I tell myself. Keep dancing.

*Now she's on her feet and takes my hands. "The lady—look.
The lady swings full circle and pivots home to face the lord." Except,
the floating—it's gone too far. It's taking me. I tighten my grip on
her hands, to try to fight it. And I—*

I am taking her.

That's why this dream's so crazy. I bring her home with me, through time.

She crashes onto my bed on her puffy landing-pad of skirts. Eyelids fluttering.

"The walls, my lady—are they shaky? Are you dizzy?"

"Yea," she says, and, "Yea."

Her feet, in their funny little duck-billed boots, don't even reach the floor.

"Try looking at just one thing," I say. "Pick any one spot and stare, till it stops moving."

When she finally speaks again, she's pointing at a poster on my wall. "What would these be? These…lutes?…that I be gazing on?" It's the one with three guitars—two of them red.

And now she frowns. "There be someone knocking."

"What?" I say.

And now she's talking, looking all around her, saying, "Mistress Ellen?"

And she's fading. Gone.

I want that dream to go on longer! That's what I remember thinking as I lay there, the *Booke of Prayre* beside me on my bed.

22 Betwixt (*preposition*: between)

Falling in love, when your friend has finally got it that she's going to die. It would make you feel split in two—even if you *weren't* still hoping for a way to save her. Even if she wasn't in another century, with time running out.

While I air-walked through the halls of Citadel High with Tom and out into the first storm of the season, pelting each other with snow, the other Jane wrote a humiliating letter to her cousin—an appeal for mercy that would get her nowhere. Then she went to a so-called trial where she didn't even get to speak. That's where the verdicts were delivered. Public execution by beheading for Guildford. Jane's royal blood earned her something (very slightly) better: when her time came—and it wouldn't be long now—she'd be beheaded on the Green in front of a small, select audience.

I'd had years of practice at feeling split in two: normal on the one hand, but walking on eggshells because of my mother. The peaceful state we'd slipped into after my trip across the bridge was holding, it seemed.

"Mom?" I tapped on her half-open study door the next Sunday. "I'm heading out to Tom's. He's—"

"*What?*" She swung her chair around. No smell of booze. But I saw it right away: the hard look in her eyes—an unfocused look that she seemed to get now sometimes, even when she wasn't drinking.

Note to self: Don't ever interrupt her when she's working.

"Guess you were right, Mom." I tried a little smile. "About Tom, I mean. You can't see the future."

"Guess you were right, Mom," she parroted back. "Don't condescend to me, Jane. I'm sick of people condescending."

Don't try to get around her with charm.

"Not to mention traipsing all over town when you don't have time to do your homework even—"

"Who says I didn't do my—"

"*Or* clean your room. You can't even see the floor in there."

"Don't go *in* there, then. Why would you—"

Don't slack off on anything. Ever.

Then her face twisted up with self-pity. "I'm sick of being the only one who lifts a finger around here. And I'm sick of people treating me like shit."

You don't deserve this. This one always required repetition: *Jane, to self: You don't deserve this.*

"Look, Mom." I shook my head as if to say, fine, have it your way. I held my hands up, palms out, and backed away over the threshold.

"Wait, Jane." Her voice went small now, suddenly pathetic. "Wait, sweetie, please," she said, and I stepped back in.

"Talk about condescending. Take a look at this." She pointed to her screen, to what wasn't work, I saw now, but her personal email. She scrolled down to the message she was answering:

You're a lovely woman, Analise. So bright and beautiful.

"What would you call that" she said, "when you're dump-
ing someone?" She read the next bit out loud, puffing her
chest out and imitating Dave's rumbly baritone:

But as I've tried to say before, your behavior is out of control
and far too unpredictable.

"My 'behavior'!" she scoffed. And I guess that's all she
meant for me to read. But I glanced down and saw the next
two lines. So cold, so formal:

I have to ask you once again to please stop contacting me.
Or I will have to consider taking legal action.

I think I gasped.

Her eyes shot up to mine—and narrowed. Her cheeks
went red with shame. "Get out of my business. Get out of
my room."

My life, she meant.

"How many times have I told you not to bother me when
I'm in my study!"

"Sorry I'm late." I was standing in Tom's porch a while later.

He shrugged. "No problem. You just missed my dad,
though. He wanted to see if you're a knockout like I told him."

Still in my boots and already blushing. *Cheek-roses*, they'd
say in Jane's time.

Tom put his arms up, elbows forward, and gripped the molding above the living room doorway like he might draw his knees up and swing from it. "Dad will catch you next time."

Next time. I peeked into the big, interconnected rooms to hide my smile. There were dark, polished floors, and textured fabrics in shades that made me think of sand and stone. Above the couch: a red silk wall hanging with a bold Asian brushstroke.

Tom's house was "Buddhagonian" from its sparse but expensive-looking furniture through to the little shrine room with the square red cushion. This reminded me of Mom's old boyfriend, Dex, who had one like it. It reminded me of Lady Jane too. Not that she had anything remotely like it. Just something to do with altars. With prayer.

The shrine room was next to Tom's bedroom, where I was soon curled up in a wicker basket chair. Strains of Justin Bieber and an occasional giggle drifted in from across the hall, and the new issue of *Citadel Scene* was spread open in my lap. "Sneak preview," Tom said. Then he fiddled with a button on his shirtsleeve while I looked for his byline.

"Nostalgia Sucks," a music essay by Tom Kantor.

CD review: "TK's Pick of the Month."

"TK?"

"Like in Tom Ka—"

I shot him a look. "But how can you write so…"

"Brilliantly?"

I glared. "I was thinking of something more specific. How can you come across so confident? You're only some kid in grade ten."

He clapped his hands over his ears. "I didn't hear that." He was on his bed, legs crossed in a lazy kind of lotus position, with a pillow scrunched underneath. *Same one he slept on every night?* A little thrill ran through me.

On the next page, Tom *again*. "Hey, you wrote that story about the Wellness Center after all." I looked up. "Tom?"

Both ears still covered.

Climbing out of a basket chair's no easy feat, at least not gracefully. But my shyness was fading.

"I'm talking to you." I stood in front of him and tried to pry his hands loose. "Mr. Teee Kaaay Kantor."

His knees were on either side of my legs. He fell backwards on the bed and I felt myself falling with him. Then—

The door flung open and a girl with wild, dark hair burst in. She looked a lot like Tom. She had a friend behind her.

"Not *again!*" Her voice was husky. "You know you can't have a girl in your room with the door shut. Not after la-ast time!" She backed away with a big whoop of laughter, and Tom was on his feet. "Sorry, Jane. Got a sister to kill." All three of them stampeded down the hall and stairs, and I could hear them bounding around the spacious rooms.

I settled on the floor and opened the paper to TK's review. Better than trying to (not) imagine "last time." It was about Arcade Fire's last release, and when Tom came back in—"She's talking crap, Jane"—I was pretty into it.

"Hey, this is good."

His face lit up. "Thanks." He flopped down on the floor across from me. "Don't know what it is about us and doors bursting open."

Us.

I felt a new attack of "cheek-roses" coming on, so I quickly stuck my head back in the paper and turned a few pages. "I like how you put this article together. 'A Day in the Life of a High School Wellness Center.' Was that your own idea?"

"Yeah."

I scanned it. Lots of talk about depression—insomnia, listlessness, dark circles under the eyes. It made me think of Jane, of course—how she would lie awake these nights, she told me, wanting to escape into a dream, but when she finally *did* fall asleep, her dreams were horrifying. And I thought about the purplish dark circles under her eyes now, as she sat glumly at the chessboard, pushing pieces around without interest.

I looked at Tom again. "'How to Help a Down Friend Up.' That's a good title for this little box."

"Thanks," he said. "Sidebar."

"Sidebar. Gotcha. But, hey"—I scanned the list of pointers—"what if they're down for a really good reason?"

"Like what?"

"Like they're going to die?"

Then—*god!* My whole body went tense, and Tom's seemed to, too. "What are you talking about, Jane? Is there something wrong with you?"

"No. No-no-no." I shook my head. It had slipped out before I could catch it. Slipped out because it was sitting there, waiting, on the tip of my tongue.

"Or—Megan? Or Crisco?"

"*No.*" And for an awful minute I couldn't think of anything. Then, "I was thinking about this book my mom's reading. That's all." (A book she *had* read once and talked about.) "It had these two characters who worked as clowns. They cheered the little kids up, on the cancer ward in a hospital."

"Little kids on the cancer ward. Sheesh."

The weight of this seemed to hang between us.

Then Tom pulled a face. "I don't think Ms. MacAllistair would look good in one of those big red noses."

And I knew I was home free.

It had a lonely side, this thing with Jane. That really hit me then. It connected me to everyone who's ever lived—like every border could be crossed and I could feel that. But it also *disconnected* me: I had something I could never tell. Then— *Hey*, I thought, *I already know that kind of loneliness; I've known it since I was a kid*. And that's what made me tell Tom one fact about my life—just one fact, but a big one—when he walked me to the bus stop later.

"You know when we were talking about my dad before?" (I had mentioned that he was killed on his motorcycle.)

Tom nodded. "Yeah?"

"Well, this was in the newspaper at the time," I started. "I didn't realize, at first. But all the grown-ups read it. Everyone."

Tom's leather-gloved fingers were entwining with my wool-gloved ones, finding a way to fit together, and I cleared my throat and told myself to carry on. After all, I wasn't going to expose her DUI conviction. Or how she sometimes crashed at her buddy Sheila's—or so she'd say. Or the time I woke up and she'd packed up half the house—smashing things while she was at it—planning to move us across the country to Tofino. Single Mother Goes Bush. "You can't do this," I remember pleading. "I start school next week." Grade seven.

Tom was still waiting.

"Well, he was on a trip to Newfoundland, my dad…"

"Uh-huh?"

"One of his nature retreats, he called them. When he'd
go off by himself…"

There was a powdering of snow beneath our feet, and
we passed a tree that was strung with blue lights—early sign
of Christmas.

"To recharge his batteries?" Tom urged me on.

"I guess." I giggled nervously. "Odd comparison to make
when you're talking about nature."

"True. He might have given me a bad mark for that, your
dad. Being an English prof."

Then it came spilling out. "Except he wasn't by himself.
There was a girl killed with him. One of his grad students
at Dal."

"Shit." Tom drew a breath in. "Pretty brutal for your
mother."

"It wasn't any picnic for me either." Just as well it was dark;
I think I glowered at him. "Like, I've just lost my dad, I'm just
a kid. And suddenly he's a bad guy, and then my mom starts…"

"What?"

"I don't know. Starts to seem far away, sometimes."

Enough. And I kept my mouth shut then. There were too
many stories rising up inside me—ones I didn't want to remember, let alone tell. Like the last time I saw my Aunt Peggy,
for one, in the funeral home parking lot. "You wrote to her
family on behalf of his?" Mom had screamed, and grabbed me
and held me in front of her like Exhibit A. "*This* is his family." She'd lifted me right off the ground for emphasis. "*This.*"

Truth, I figured, was like potato chips or chocolate. (Talk
about an odd comparison.) It's hard to stop with just one piece.

23 Abyssm (*noun*: abyss, chasm, gulf)

That night, I heard Mom's boot heels tapping down the hallway. Her black suede boots; I knew the sound. All the rules, like No Shoes in the House, turned to smoke when Analise was heading for a bender. The back door slammed, and then her old Volvo *chup-chupped* into gear.

I flicked my light on after a while, and lay there staring at the ceiling. I couldn't concentrate to read. Couldn't turn on my music, not with one ear cocked in case she came back. And Tom. Couldn't think about Tom. He was like a gift. And if a gift got unwrapped in this atmosphere, the sweetness and excitement might get contaminated.

My comforter was wrapped around me, snug, and I was wearing my softest sweatshirt and new pajama bottoms (khaki, with a strip of white piping). But this room was no haven. Just a box, so small you could suffocate. The rest of the house was hers. Foreign territory. Enemy terrain. And she really could come back at any point (or not), from the Atlantica or wherever, on her own or with some random drinking buddies in tow.

If only I could drift off to sleep, like I could drift from my century to Jane's and back. Sometimes I wondered how that looked to her: when I'd hear something calling me and suddenly be—*gone*. Just like *she* had suddenly been gone, I thought, in that dream I'd had.

In the end I got the prayer book from my drawer. One of the most comforting things ever was just to look at it and hold it. It really took me someplace—in the figure-of-speech way, I mean. It fell open to a page with an illuminated letter *O*. A swirl of curlicues. No clear path in or out. A maze.

What can I do, my lady? Is there some way I can save you? Is there somehow a parallel universe where you could get to live your life? Are you holding this book too, right now?

Can we both be?

I decided to go.

Everything was black.

Was time unwinding faster? Had it all—had it happened already?

I felt colder than I remembered feeling.

Jane?

Then—"Our father who art in heaven, hallowed be thy…"

And a glimmer of light was starting to seep in.

"Let thy kingdom come, for thy will be fulfilled…"

Was it moonlight?

"In earth as it is in heaven…"

Earth.

We *were* on Earth, still.

It was her room. I could just make out the outline of the window now, and a thread of light across the floor.

I couldn't make out Jane's shape, but I knew she was

kneeling at her bed in the farthest corner. That's where her voice was coming from.

"...and forgive our offense, like as we do forgive them..."

This wasn't right—listening in on her. But before I could speak up, she switched from the memorized prayer to her own words—way more urgent.

"How long wilt thou be absent?" Her voice was just this side of breaking. "Forever? Is thy mercy clean gone?"

It was my mother at my door that brought me home.

"Jane? You awake in there?"

I couldn't move my mind that fast.

"Jane?"

I was *not* ready for this.

She kept knocking louder, but stopped short of barging in. Single Mother Shows Some Respect.

"I only had a couple of drinks tonight."

That was good. But was I supposed to say, *Congratulations*?

"Are you sleeping, sweetie?"

I felt like she could hear me breathe. I made a sleepy noise, like, "Go'way."

"I stopped for you," she said. "Because of you, Jane."

I'd heard that before. I actually used to think she meant something by it.

"Can I come in? For just a sec?" She sounded almost like a kid.

After what I had just overhead tonight, her need for reassurance didn't cut it. I inched closer to the wall and stuck my head under my pillow.

"Are you sleeping?"
I stayed there, hardly breathing, till she finally went away.

24 Scape (*verb*: escape, avoid)

Jane was glumly setting up the chessboard the next day; me sitting across from her. Her eyes seemed even more intense now, and larger in her face—I figured she wasn't eating much. The headdress she was wearing had a stiff little bonnet sewn in—her own personal pitched roof. Too bad it couldn't give her shelter. How many days did she have left? I knew her execution date—February 12—but with the days moving faster here, I wasn't sure what date we were *on* exactly. And did I *want* to know?

"Wilt thou sacrifice thyself for me?"

"I—pardon?"

Then I saw that she was talking to a pawn, held in the palm of her hand. "If a pawn can make it to the other side, a queen shall have new life. Shall I dispatch thee thus? Or, mayhap"—her eyes narrowed—"that works only for a rightful queen?"

That play—it's called "promotion"—works only when the queen's been killed already. But I'd hardly remind her of this.

"Feckenham."

I thought she was swearing at first. "What?"

"Father Feckenham. Her Grace my cousin's personal advisor on all things…holy. She is sending him to try to convert

183

me." She put the pawn down. "Howsoever shall I suffer it? To think of him here in my chamber with that great mawkish crucifix about his neck!"

I took a breath. I decided to break my promise—the one I'd made after our fight that time—and make the argument she hated: "If he *did* convert you—"

"He shan't."

"But is there still a chance—"

She cut me off again. "'Tis true," she said. "In all likelihood I *could* yet trade my eternal life for a longer spell of this one."

What to say to that? I fiddled with my little ivory queen. Picked her up. Put her back beside her royal husband.

"Namesake?"

"Yes?"

"Do you not know I *want* to live, the same as anyone?"

A mouse skittered in the eaves somewhere and a log shifted in the fire, collapsing in on itself.

"Pray, tell me a tale," she said after a few minutes. She had her queen gripped in one fist now, and gestured with her absentmindedly. "A tale of your flying machines or horseless carriages. Distract me, I prithee."

That's what I was becoming more and more: a distraction. Something almost dreamlike to her; I could feel that. A kind of escape.

Escape. It kept repeating in my head.

I looked down at the empty square Jane's queen had left behind.

I leaned in close—"you should escape from here"—and Jane pulled back: "However could I?"

"That," I said, "is what we have to figure out."

"There be no way on God's earth—"

"I could help," I said. Maybe *that's* what I was here for. "I could—I don't know—throw things around and make noise while you sneak out. And—"

"Nay. It be sheer madness."

"Come on," I said. "Just humor me. Say there *was* a way—where would you want to go?"

"To go?" she said at last. "If you persist in speaking foolishness, to Bradgate. If you could see it, Jane, the wooded hills." But then she raised a hand as if to block out the image. "I shall never go home again. The fate that both my parents set for me my father has now sealed. Heaven help me, to think my life will soon be shortened by the very one whose seed began it."

It wasn't the first time she'd said this, or the first time my sympathetic murmuring seemed like a lame response. *Why didn't I think of it before? All I have to do is get her out of here.* I was on my feet now, pacing—from poky little window to poky fire to scratchy bed to trunk in the dark corner. My mind jumped to the caged lions Mr. Gregor had mentioned, in the Royal Menagerie—and from Lord Grey to my own father. When he betrayed my mother did he betray me too? *Why didn't I think of* this *before, either?* Didn't want to believe they'd *both* screwed up on me?

Small-time screw-ups though, compared...

"We still have time," I said, "to get you somewhere safe. And I'll go too. I can help you find your way."

"Have you lost your senses? What if something calls you home?"

"Well, I'll just come back. Fast as I can."

"Hours could pass, between. In my time."

"Yeah." That did sound scary. "Not days, though. At least we know *that*."

"Where would we fetch up, pray?"

"I don't know," I said. "Some village. Anyplace where there'd be farmers, workers, you know, people to mix in with. We'd have to find you clothes." It hit me—"Hey, *I* could bring clothes."

"You *could*?"

"Yeah. There are places in my time where they have costumes. Things like people wear right now."

"That commoners wear?"

"Uh-huh."

She frowned down at my jeans. "And they look real?"

"They do," I said. "I've seen them used in plays. Neptune Theatre," I said. "Downtown. I bet they rent them there."

She took a breath. The room went quiet for a minute— just a bit of snap 'n' crackling from the grate. And when she spoke again, I knew she wasn't just playing along with me.

"There are some who *have* been known to slip through the Tower gates disguised as workers. If you could bring me garments"—her words were measured and her voice a whisper—"no one here would need be party to it. No one here would need take that risk."

We looked at each other, her eyes brightening and mine probably clouding with doubt. Scary—now that it sounded real. But I remembered it was her only chance.

"How would I declare myself?"

"Declare yourself?"

"Folks might believe I was cast out from my village," she said, "for ill-doing. Black magic. Or take me for a carrier. A woman with no past to lay a claim to, 'tis a sound enow assumption." She held her huge sleeve up and tapped her inner wrist. "'Tis here, where they would look to find the red ring of the sweating sickness or the black boils of the Plague."

"But they wouldn't find them."

"Nay? By times, I wonder what *is* written in your history books. People oft-times see what they set out to see. Or fear most."

"We'll just have to make up something really good."

Jane was on her feet now too, both of us pacing the low-ceilinged room. "Let's find a name for you, to start. What will we call you?" And she answered right away. "I have always fancied that I should like to be called Matilda."

"*Matilda?*" I stopped in mid-step.

"Do you think it seems…too fair for me?"

"No way. It sounds old-fashioned, that's all. You *are* fair. Matilda who? What will your last name be?"

She smiled. "Not Anjou, for certes."

"Huh?"

"I speak of *Queen* Matilda?"

"Never heard of her."

"Queen Matilda and her bold escape?"

We were both standing by the fire. "'Twas the year of our Lord eleven hundred forty-two," Jane said. "A bitter year, so cold the Thames was frozen over. Queen Matilda was imprisoned in her castle, by her cousin, Stephen. He would not see England ruled by a mere woman.

"But she escaped," she said. "The good queen made her way across the Thames—on foot. 'Twas snowing hard that night." She touched my arm. "She crept past all the sentries in her nightshirt. Her *white* nightshirt. Under cover of the falling snow."

"She made it? That's amazing! So will you."

But Jane's eyes dimmed then and she turned away.

"The rest of the story comes to me, to caution me." Her skirts rustled as she reached for the iron poker. "She had allies, Queen Matilda." She sifted through the coals, and for a minute the fire burned hot and bright. "Half her subjects were loyal to Stephen and half to her. For me, there would be no one rising up. No rider waiting on the far side with a mount for me, at the ready."

"That's why we'll give you a new name, a new identity."

She gave the fire another stir, but not much came of it. "'Tis sheer folly," she said, "to even think on it. Akin to..." She stopped, not wanting, I figured, to mention my disaster in London.

London. "In London, it would be easier to blend in with the crowd."

She shuddered. "Nay—the cold, flat look in people's eyes that day my barge sailed past St. Paul's. *Who be this Queen Jane, thrust upon us?* Me with those chopines strapped to my feet so they could see me. The way they looked at me has put me clean off crowds. *And* London."

While I tried to think what to say next, footsteps sounded on the stairs. The door inched open. Mistress Ellen.

Time to sup was *nigh*, she said. Her lady *must needs eat* to keep her strength up. But her eyes were red-rimmed, and I didn't believe she thought Jane needed strength for much.

She went into the next room, and we could hear her shuffling around. And then, of all things, the wobbly strains of a song came through. The one about the harvest queen:

"I brought thee ke-erchers to thy he-ad
that we-ere wrought fi-ine and gallantly..."

"How can she do that? Sing?"

Jane seemed surprised. "Because she knows it soothes me. You might be well advised to do the same."

"What? Have you ever *heard* me?"

Glint of a smile then—like the coals just stirred. "Sing not," she said. "But bring me comfort. All this talk of escape—it only lifts me up to cast me down again." She pulled her shoulders straight and looked away. "My prayer," she said, "is that the axeman will be skilled and will dispatch me quickly. Oh, in my worst of dreams..."

And then she turned and looked at me. "I had one *joyful* dream of late. 'Twas all too brief. I meant to tell you. I came to your world. I was being air-drawn. You were with me, Namesake, pulling me along.

"Then I was gazing at a painting—or a hanging? There were two red lutes," she said, "as I recall it."

25 Penning (*noun*: handwriting)

Possibility #1: Jane really had come to my world. Possibility #2: It was just coincidence; we'd had the same kind of dream. Possibility #3 (a variation): It was a dream, but through some kind of psychic connection, she was able to see one of the posters on my wall. These days, I'd hardly call *anything* impossible. Except for—

*Im*possibility #1: that *this* was where she could escape to—my world. I *did* think that for one exciting minute. Then I remembered that she'd quickly been called back. Same rules for both of us. And, besides, an invisible person can't have a life.

The whole thing kept running through my head—how Jane had taken hold of my hands to show me those dance steps. If it *was* real, that's how it must have happened. I started running through it again as soon as I woke up the next morning.

"Jane, are you coming down for breakfast?" my mother hollered up the stairs. She was down there making happy domestic noises, trying so hard that I couldn't help but soften toward her, a bit. "Shall I pop in some toast for you?" Like toast was highly delightful. Jane would call her "valiant" in her "good cheer."

"Thanks, Mom," I called, "but I'm having a shower first."
I couldn't face all that neediness. I made my shower so long
and luxuriant that when it was finished she was singing out,
"Good-bye!"

I cracked the door open. "Have a great day, Mom!" I
shouted through the steam. Stay on the wagon! I didn't say
that part, though I did cross my fingers for her—for both of
us—hoping she would.

In my room, my Citadel High agenda winked at me from
under a pile of clothes and papers (Mom was right: I had aban-
doned my usual tidiness, with so much going on). I stepped
over it and realized: no way was I going to school today. Not
with only a few chances left, I figured, to ever see Jane. I got
dressed, blew my hair dry, and reached into my night table
drawer for the book.

But this time—for the first time—Jane didn't want to see me
when I got there. She was sitting on her bed with Mistress
Ellen, the two of them slumped together, holding on to each
other. Jane's head was bare, her hair pushed back and tangled.
She blinked when she noticed me, and gave a wan little smile.
I felt like an intruder, like I'd felt that one other time—the
visit she never knew about.

And Mistress Ellen—her features seemed all folded in on
themselves. This was grief, before the fact. I knew what grief
looked like, so I headed down the steep stone staircase to the
Green—to give it the privacy it deserved.

There was a soft layer of snow, and a few new flakes falling.
People were coming and going, but it all seemed like slow

motion. Everything subdued. Was it the snow—the way snow
muffles things? Or—I thought of an expression my mom had
used when some of the office staff at her university were being
laid off: "Everyone's just waiting for the ax to fall." The stuff
we say, not even getting it.

I nearly collided with two women crossing the Green—
ladies' maids, judging by the smooth wool of their cloaks.

"They say Queen Mary's fancy priest is being sent to talk
to her," one of them said. "The new Abbot of Westminster.
Mayhap he can bring her around."

The other woman shook her head. "Nary a chance. Not
with her so loyal to the New Faith."

"The ground we tread, then—it be set to hold the scaffold."

I went back again later but the priest was there by then. I
returned to Jane's world a few more times through the day—
and he was still there, always, the two of them talking. The
wooden cross that hung around his neck *was* large, as Jane
had predicted, and set with jewels. And his white gown was
stitched with what I assumed were threads of gold.

He didn't seem pompous though; he seemed intelligent
and gentle. His gray-blue eyes were fixed on Jane's as she
talked, his hands moving in response, coming together at
the fingertips, while Jane, practically glowing with intensity,
gave her views about different verses in the Bible. She looked
interested, though definitely skeptical, when *he* talked. "By
what scripture find you that?" I heard her pounce on him at
one point, just as my alarm went off.

What a weird, long day. I kept resetting my alarm. Going back and forth again. I didn't eat. My stomach felt too quivery. Didn't answer my phone, not even texts from Tom. I couldn't settle down in either world, so how could I come off seeming normal?

At one point I tried to distract myself by cleaning my room, but I couldn't concentrate on that either. I ended up standing there with my shoebox full of ticket stubs and souvenirs in one hand, and a blouse that needed ironing in the other. I didn't know where to turn, so I just put them back on the floor.

And what a long night. Even longer and more…hollow because Mom didn't show up after work. Surprising, kind of. She had seemed so determined. Either something had tipped things in the wrong direction—some snarky crack from a student, maybe—or she just got weak. That's what I was thinking as the clock passed midnight. I was lying there, still dressed, on top of my comforter, in that particular kind of quiet that happens only in an empty house. *Something might have tipped things in the wrong direction. She might not blow in until tomorrow.*

Since I couldn't sleep, I reached into my drawer for the prayer book. A new day in Jane's world; would the priest be gone? The book felt perfect in my hands, like always. The pages soft and creamy. I turned a few, just to look at it first, like I often did. But then—

What was *this*?

There was handwriting. Across the bottom of two pages.

Forasmuche as you… it started.

Who did this? Not my *mother*, surely?

No. It wasn't regular writing. It was writing from then. Like Jane's. Exactly like Jane's writing in her letter to Edward Seymour.

Why hadn't I noticed it before?

Forasmuche as you have desired

so simple a woman to wrighte

in so worthy a booke,

gode mayster Lieuftenante

therefore I shalle as a frende...

Jane was writing this for the lieutenant, John Bridges? Right. I *had* read that she gave him—I swallowed—gave him her prayer book as a souvenir. Like prisoners did before they...

Of course I didn't see this before. It wasn't there until now.

26   Air-drawn (*adjective*: drawn through the air; or: drawn in the air)

She was still there at least. She was standing by the fire when I arrived, and I came right out with it. "How long do you have left?"

She glanced at me and then away. She tugged one by one at the fingertips of her white gloves. Outside on the Green, someone was tapping, tapping. *Hammering.*

"Pray, did you see Queen Mary's priest?" she asked, instead of answering me. Then—"Yea, you *did*. I saw you—thrice. He be a gentle man, a good man. Not at all as I anticipated."

"So? Is there any chance?" *Of course there wasn't.* But when Jane's eyes met mine, I didn't see any hint of anger about my question. Her eyes weren't bloodshot either. Not like Mistress Ellen's. Above the purplish shadows, they were like her voice—clear, strangely calm.

"Father Feckenham has asked if he might stand with me," she said, "to join me in my final prayer. And I have bid him do so. 'Twill be"—she looked straight at me—"on the morrow." And that's when her composure crumbled. She pressed her hands over her ears to try to block out the hammering. "That infernal sound! Is there no way I can be spared it? Can I find no scape? No shelter?"

There was nothing I—or anyone—could do for her.

Except—my alarm was set to go off soon. Maybe I could do one thing. However tiny.

"Here, take my hands," I told her when I heard the ringing—just when the floating was about to start. "Hold tight. Let's hope this works," I said. "Get ready for a good dream."

It was like being at a beach, at the water's edge.

I was aware this time, while it was happening—

The tide strong, the undertow...

Trying to pull me out to sea and I could feel all the grains of sand around me going with it. But it was air that I was fighting back against, not water, not the ground at my feet. The air my hands were reaching through. Holding her hands so I could bring her...

With me.

When my eyes cleared and the world had stopped shaking, Jane was staring at one of my posters, like before. She gave me a quick, woozy look, then focused straight ahead again. "I have found one spot to gaze on, as you bid me do the other time." Such an amazing student—even of her own dreams. Or so-called dreams. Why hadn't I got it that this was real? Because the moving back and forth was *always* dreamlike? As for Jane, she'd been sleeping at the start of it, that other time.

"Hey, wait. Don't move," I told her. Not that she was likely to. I dashed down the hall to my mother's room. No Mom. Looked out her window to the lane. It looked like morning out there. Daylight, anyway. No car.

When I returned, Jane was still staring at the poster, and I stood back and did some staring too.

I thought of something we had learned in Science. About cyclones, of all things. How they rip through whatever's in their path, but leave everything around it untouched. My room looked just like always—a regular twenty-first-century room—only here was this living, breathing person from another time, with the color coming back into her cheeks.

Her big sleeves and skirts seemed even more dramatic here, and her headdress—the one like a roof. And she'd brought a trace of wood smoke, and of rosewater.

"Namesake?" She pointed at the poster. "What did you say these were again? Or did you?"

"Electric guitars," I said. "A bit like lutes."

"And what would they be *made* with?" She looked eager to make sense of this—of something. "What manner of paint," she asked, "so flat..."

"It's a photo. Remember, like I told you about?" I'd once told her the story of Princess Diana and the paparazzi, and then wished I hadn't; it had made her look pretty sad. "That's what most of these are." I swept my hand to take in all my posters. "But not the lion." I pointed at Aslan. "That's a painting. Well, a photograph of a painting."

Was she starting to look paler again? Or maybe a bit green?

I reminded myself that I hadn't been able to take in the whole White Tower at first. I'd focused on the big black door. And Odin.

God—the prayer book. It would be way too weird for Jane to see it. I glanced down. It was peeking out where my comforter had slid partly onto the floor. I shoved it under the bed with my toe. *Sorry*, I said under my breath.

Jane was looking around now—slow, but curious. I gave her hand a reassuring pat. After a few minutes I pointed to my bulletin board, behind her. "I'll show you some more pictures. Photographs, I mean. These ones are from my own life."

I knelt on the bed and helped her kneel beside me. It was complicated, getting all those layers of skirt arranged so she wouldn't slip around, and we ended up laughing. Our first laugh in this world—and I noticed that hers had a lightness, a kind of lilt to it—and her face looked bright and open. That was the great thing about "dreams." In a dream you're not awaiting execution; you're not stuck in the Tower, or aware that something will zap you back there at any minute. You're just experiencing what comes in.

"Here's Megan and Traci." I pointed to the bikini shot. "Here's a picture of my dad."

Her eyes scanned the board. "Is your mother among them?"

"No. She's right here in the house, I don't need *her* picture." Then I wondered, had that ever hurt her feelings? I could ask her for one. I felt a small surge of hope about our relationship—well, starting whenever she turned up.

"She be here now?" asked Jane.

"No, she's…" Passed out somewhere? Sobering up? Still drinking? Dangling by a thread. I crossed my fingers, hoping for her. "She's out."

Jane was looking at my dad's wallet-sized photo, and then at me. "I do declare, thine eyes and smile are akin to thy father's."

"I bet that's why they call it 'a-kin'." I nudged her. "Get it?"

"Daresay I do."

"Do you really think so?"

"Verily."

I looked down at my little dad. His eyes were blue, not gray like mine. But the same dark lashes. And there *was* something similar—a sort of shyness—in our smiles.

"Hmmn," I said. "And people used to say I looked like his sister, my Aunt Peggy. Here's the two of them, in their teens."

Jane tilted her head. "Do you have a photograph of her now?"

"No. I haven't seen her in a long time."

"Does she live afar?"

"No." I actually knew from Internet snooping that she and Kate had moved into Halifax from the country a couple of years ago; they lived near Crisco's house. "My mom cut off all contact. Family argument," I said, and Jane hardly seemed surprised by such a concept. She looked at my dad again, and back at me. "Lo, you have the same long jawline."

"Thanks. I guess." I rubbed my chin. "You don't mean like Mistress Tilney's?"

"Get away!" she said. "You are comely. Not to speak ill of Mistress Tilney's features."

"No. No way. Hey, will you listen to us? Talk about ste-reotypical teenage girls. I've got the whole *world* to show you, and we're talking about our looks."

"Ster-eo? Typ-ical..."

"I'll explain it later. Oh, my lady! This just blows my mind."

"It...pardon?"

"I'll explain that too."

Then, out of the corner of my eye, I noticed my back-pack in the corner, slumped on top of my library books and mostly hiding them (one advantage of a messy room). But one corner of *The Nine Days Queen* was sticking out—what a way to spoil Jane's dream. "Hey," I said brightly, "let me show you the rest of the house."

"But there be much to see right here in your own chamber."

"No! I mean, I'm hungry," I said, urging her to follow me. And it struck me that this was true.

A few feet down the hall Jane stopped and stared into the bathroom.

"That's just the privy."

"Nay!" She took a step inside, and I tried to see it through her eyes. Gleaming white fixtures. Fluffy towels. The clawfoot tub my mom had painted a deep sea green.

"Did you not say you were a commoner?"

"I am."

"Then everyone in your world must live as kings."

"No, not at all." I started to point out that our house was no castle, but Jane was distracted, staring into her own face.

"Never have I spied myself in a glass so large." She frowned and looked closer. "These shadows underneath my eyes."

"That's just because you're not getting enough sleep." Then I moved on, not wanting to remind her of reality. "Look." I waved to indicate the two of us in the mirror. "Me so gangly, and you petite."

She raised an eyebrow. "Be this not *story-o-predictable?*"

My mouth fell open. "You just nailed it. You're such a brainiac. So smart. Let's go downstairs," I told her.

"Prithee, lead the way."

As the living room and hallway unfolded below us, it hit me that nothing flowed or billowed. No tapestries, no velvet, no

shimmering candlelight from wall sconces: the stuff she would
be used to until recently. But my mother's streamlined kitch-
en was an amusement park and Jane and I had tickets. The
fridge—she backed away at first, "yon cold coffin of light."
The garburator, which freaked her out too. The amazement
of hot running water. Then she found the Lazy Susan full of
spice jars, took the lid off each one, reverently, and sniffed.
"Be this cardamom? Cayenne? Are you *certain* you be a commoner?" *The great search for the Spice Route.* I'd brought her to
a New World in more ways than one.

At one point we stood at the window, looking out at
the yards and the back lane. No snow; this was a gray-brown
patch of winter. But things looked peaceful and contained: a
gang of chickadees at someone's birdfeeder, bushes wrapped
in burlap in a yard across the lane, garbage cans lined up neatly
for pick-up. "Cars," I said, pointing to Mrs. Lynde's red Toyota
and a couple of others that were parked nearby—the horseless
carriages I'd described to her, as her tutor.

We went outside then (good thing Jane didn't need a coat,
I thought; her bell sleeves would never fit in one). We headed
to Needham Hill so she could see the harbor and the city sky-
line. All was quiet on Stairs Place—but we'd crossed Novalea
Drive and were just starting up the hill when a light must have
changed. Traffic came streaming in both directions. Jane, who
was behind me and had stopped to look back, gathered her skirts
as best she could and tried to scramble up the bumpy slope.

"They set upon me—to run me down!"

"No, my lady. They can't even *see* you."

She came to a stop. But her breath was shallow and her
forehead creased.

"Look." I pointed down at the now-thinning traffic. "*They don't leave the street.*"

"Where…do they go?" The #7 bus rolled by then and she grabbed my arm. "Who would they all be, Jane?"

"Just people. Just going wherever."

"At such a speed?"

"That's how fast things go now."

"It must be frightening to live in this time."

"Not really," I said with a shrug. (I'd never told her about the state of the planet.)

We came to the top of the hill and looked down. Office towers in the distance; Jane couldn't believe how tall. Ships in the harbor; she couldn't believe how ugly, without sails.

"How do they move?"

I didn't know, specifically. "Some type of engine."

Two ships—a gray Navy ship and a rusty-looking freighter—crossed paths below us in the Narrows. The cars crossing the MacKay Bridge delighted her—safely miniaturized by distance. So did the colorful wooden houses on the streets that sloped down to the water.

"'Tis strange. Yet, aside from the ships," she said, "it be passing beautiful."

I noticed that her teeth were chattering. "Are you cold, still? We should go in," I said.

Back in the house—my mother still not home—I remembered again that I was hungry. "Come on. It's time you were introduced to a true classic of my time: peanut butter and jam."

She liked the peanut butter—"tasty, though vexatious to chew"—and she spread the jam on thick. I figured the textbooks were right about people in her world being sugar addicts. Apparently Shakespeare, a few years later, ate so much of it his teeth turned black.

I took my plate to the sink, and when I glanced back Jane was following with hers, making a detour around the butcher block, dark skirts sweeping across the black and white tiles.

"If a pawn can make it to the other side, a queen shall have new life."

"Who would that be? Your mother?"

"What?"

The front door was visible from where Jane was standing. I leaned over to look. *Mrs. Lynde.*

"Shit. She sees me. I'll have to answer. This will only take a second."

She's looking right at me and thinks I'm talking to myself. I pasted on a smile and went to greet her.

"Hi," I said, and then, "thanks," since she had a jar of jelly in her hands. Quince, from a bush in her backyard. It was another tradition, like the zucchini baby on the doorstep. "But didn't you already—"

"I just noticed I had extra." Her smile showed a row of long teeth, and the pale red of the jelly matched the beret that was perched above her curls.

She looked past me, nosily.

"My mom's not home."

"No, of course not, dear. Her car's gone."

That seemed to have slipped out accidentally.

"That is truly an amazing outfit."

"Oh?" I looked down at my jeans and sweater. New, but no big deal. "It was on sale at Le Château."

"My dear, I hardly think so. Aren't you going to—"

to get back to Jane. "I *am* going to school," I said. "Any minute now. We had a spare, we had a *couple* of spares—"

"No. Aren't you going to introduce me to your friend?"

"My…friend?"

The jar of jelly was still in her hands, and I watched my hands reach out and take it. I watched them place it on the hall table, where it wouldn't slip and smash. I heard the rustle of Jane's skirts as she came forward to be introduced. It was the only thing to do, it seemed. I watched her curtsey.

"This is…" What to *call* her? And I couldn't think of Mrs. Lynde's name either. Not her real one.

"This is my neighbor," I ended up mumbling. "And this is my friend. My friend Matilda." I watched a totally joyful smile spread across Jane's face. "She's rehearsing for a play."

Mrs. Lynde's quick, bobbing nod seemed to say, *well, obviously.*

"It looks so real," she said to Jane, "your outfit. Just like on that mini-series."

Jane smiled like she understood.

"Wherever did you get it?"

"Why, 'twas made for me," she said, and I said, "Neptune."

"Would you spin around for me? Oh, look at that head-dress! And the skirt so full. I can't imagine how you put it on."

"Mistress Ellen always laces me."

"The wardrobe mistress," I threw in, "at Neptune." Though Mrs. Lynde was pretty much ignoring me by now.

By the time I got her out of there, saying I'd be late for class, she had complimented every stitch of clothing Jane had on. And her posture. "You hold yourself perfectly. If I didn't know better, I'd think you *were* a member of a royal court."

I couldn't see Jane's face right then. What a mix of emotions must have crossed it.

"Your accent needs some work. But you'll do fine, dear." She turned to leave, then glanced back over her shoulder with a conspiratorial wink. "Just keep practicing. I know you'll get it."

I don't remember what happened first. Did we burst out laughing about Jane's accent, or look at each other in shock?

"She could see me."

"She could see you, yeah. She must have…psychic abilities." *But* her? *Hard to imagine.*

"The way the beasts can see. That wee dog you told me of, who licked your hand."

"And Odin." *Let's not forget Odin.* Or…a kernel of a thought twigged in my mind, but slipped away before I could catch it.

Then something swept across Jane's face—a half-here half-gone look like she must have seen on mine so often. *No, not yet.* But I knew it for what it was. I could even hear her talking on the other side. "*Mistress Ellen* …" Her voice faded as her image disappeared. As fast as a screen goes blank.

27 Beckoning (*noun*: signal, significant gesture, meaningful sign)

For a while I just stood in the kitchen—sniffing around, to be precise, to catch a lingering scent of rosewater. I caught it. *That was real. That happened.*

The landline rang and I grabbed it without thinking.

"Jane?" It was Megan. "Where have you got to? What have you done with your phone? Like, have you disappeared?"

"No, Meg. I'm just not feeling good."

"You sick?"

"Not...really."

"Listen, can you come downtown?" I heard a surge of traffic through the phone and a truck backing up, beeping. "I'm heading to Spring Garden to meet Crisco at the Second Cup. I was off all morning at the dentist's—*yuk*—and she keeps texting me. She's worried because you weren't in History—"

"*Worried?*"

"Search me. She says she needs to talk to you."

"What for?"

"Like I said, I don't know. But can you meet us?"

"No, I don't think."

The cannon on Citadel Hill started booming out the hour—twelve noon. Loud, even through the phone. "C'mon," said Megan, when the twelfth boom faded. "If you leave right now you can catch the #7..." In the end I caved. I looked around the room and felt something big and painful welling up. I didn't want to be alone right now.

Meg must have made a detour, because I got to the Second Cup first. I got a coffee—being tired, all of a sudden—and was taking my first sip when they came striding in together in their army boots and bomber jackets, Crisco in artfully torn jeans. Meg was wrapping up a phone call, making smoochy sounds to Simon.

"Hey, Jane." Crisco sank into the chair across from me. She was chomping on a wad of gum.

Meg pulled up another chair and we both looked at Crisco, who took a breath and dove in.

"Are you in shit?"

"What do you mean?" I asked her.

"Last night. I thought I might have gotten you in trouble. I tried to call you but your phone was off."

"Your phone's off half the time these days," said Megan, and I looked down at my coffee. *There'll be no more need of that now.*

"Your mother was in the store."

I sighed. *Another make-up gift?* Though the Black Market was more Crisco's style, or Meg's. "Did she buy anything?"

"Uh-uh." Crisco was unzipping her jacket, and my stomach flipped. That sweater—it went well with any hair color, even mustard like hers. And topped with chunky beads on a strand of twine, it looked nearly funky.

"You weren't wearing that then?"

She closed her eyes, then nodded. "You *are* allowed to give your own clothes away. Right?"

"Sure." I tried to sound casual. "And anyhow, we could just happen to have the same sweater."

"Well, me and my big mouth." She started pulling on her fingers one by one, until a knuckle popped. "Oh, sorry." She flattened both hands on the table and leaned forward, her kohl-rimmed eyes looking straight into mine. "Your mom said 'what a beautiful sweater,' right?"

I nodded.

"She said, 'Jane has one just like it.' And I said, 'Not anymore she doesn't. She gave it to Megan, but her boobs were too big.'"

I just looked at her. "You told her that I gave away..."

"Yeah. And that Meg gave it to me. She seemed kind of, I don't know..." She blew a bubble and looked down to watch its progress.

"Insulted?"

It burst, and she roped it back in with her tongue. "Well, more like...stricken. It was awful, Jane. I didn't realize. I'm sorry."

Fair enough, I thought. "It wasn't your fault."

"She was looking at some earrings. The exact same color, now I think of it. And she just threw them on the counter. Like, literally. They hit the floor. And she ran out."

I felt my breath rush out. I looked away from Crisco's pained blue eyes and Megan's sympathetic green ones. I felt a surge of pity for my mother; Crisco had thought she was so cool. And shame came next. For both of us. For—*who knows?*—everything. What hit me last was fear. Crisco was right to warn me. Hell *would* Break Loose.

She got up then, still fidgeting, to go get coffee. And silence fell. *Be the great friend that you are, Meg. Don't say how good it is to finally have* something, *at least, in the open.* And I couldn't think of anything normal to say to change the subject. My neighbor having "the gift of sight"—that wouldn't cut it.

Crisco came back and she and Megan got talking. Light stuff. Filler. Then Megan reached into her bag. She pulled out her hand mirror, to reapply her lip gloss, and it was like some string had been pulled and tightened all my senses. Like the sun gathered up its light and tossed it down to me. I caught it.

I got up so fast I nearly knocked my chair over.

"Are you okay?"

I reached back to grab the chair, still staring at the mirror, which Meg held out to me with a puzzled look. "Did you want to *use* this?"

"No," I said. "No. There's something I just realized. I've gotta go." *Sound normal, Jane.* "I've got to go home and…get ready for my mother."

Crisco was on her feet. "Should we come with you?"

"No!" I said. Then, "Thanks, though."

A smile was rising up; it was going to break out all over me—might lift me off the ground. "I'll meet you guys after school," I told them. "Tomorrow. At the Bell Road door."

Maybe true, I thought, as I headed up Spring Garden. And maybe not. I'd probably text them later with some excuse, to put things off a bit more. But when I did see them next, I'd be introducing them to a new friend.

28 Rent (*adjective*: torn, shredded, ripped up)

She can live here, she can have a life. That kept playing in my head as I walked home. My excitement carried me faster than the #7 could have. No vehicle could have contained me.

Of course my snoopy neighbor didn't have psychic ability or some special "sight." Jane wasn't *invisible* here. It wasn't the same as when *I* went to *her* world. I should have got that the minute she looked in the mirror—and saw her reflection. And I saw it too. When I stood with that long-nosed barrister at the London market stall, looking into mirrors, my reflection wasn't there.

That's what had been at the edge of my mind, what I couldn't put my finger on. Now it all fell into place. That's why Mrs. Lynde came over with her so-called extra jar of jelly: she'd seen us walking up the street and thought, *Who's that?* That's why Jane was cold up on the hill. She had a real body here—one that actually felt the temperature, instead of just catching initial impressions and morphing around them, or whatever. Jane was like the prayer book itself—she could be in both places.

This was her parallel universe. This was her escape.

I rubbed my upper arms through the fabric of my peacoat. I'd brought her here—pretty strong arms.

Why were the rules different for the two of us? Because Jane was from the past, and the past was real, here, already, but I was from the future—and the future *wasn't* real there? Didn't my mother say visiting the past is one thing, and visiting the future another? No—*seeing*, she must have said, not visiting! Anyway, I didn't want to let *her* in.

Needham Hill came into view. *As soon as I get home, Jane, I'm coming to get you.* Not tomorrow. Tomorrow would be too late.

My lady—I imagined what I'd say to her. *The twenty-first century* is *a scary place in some ways, but it's, well, better lit.* We could make a room for her in the attic, like Megan's room, where she could see the stars—same stars she'd know already— and watch the clouds drift by. I'd even give her my room if she'd rather, and I could move up there. *You'll like Megan,* I'd say. *She's so smart. I know you'll just love talking to her. You'll like Traci too. And Tom, I'm so glad you'll get to know him.* And my mom—somehow we'd have to explain the whole truth to her. We could do that together. *A lot of the time, my lady, she really is okay.* And, hey, I thought, it will be two of us against one now.

A gust of wind hit me when I turned onto Stairs Place, and it seemed to be carrying words:

She can only stay until something calls her home again.

But I had words to throw back at it. Textbook words that happened to be true:

Without the portal, no travel through time can occur.

Once Jane was safely here—once it had done its final work—I would have to destroy the prayer book. Put it through my mother's paper shredder? Burn it in the woodstove? Almost unbearable to think of. But I'd have to do it right away.

When I arrived, I eased the door shut behind me. If Mom was home by now and passed out, I needed her to stay that way. *Lady Jane, meet Analise. You'll like her fine once she stops shouting and foaming at the mouth.* Bad start.

We'll tell everyone at school you're my cousin from England, I kept rehearsing as I tiptoed across the living room, *my long-lost cousin. Your parents got killed in a car accident and—*

At the foot of the stairs, I saw a mix CD that Tom had burned for me. And a pile of stuff beside it. Hair clips. A video card. I turned it over. *Mine.*

All the way up the stairs were little pieces of my life. The Habs baseball cap that lived on the head of my old teddy bear. My *Brownie* pin? A friendship bracelet: *Jane and Theresa, 4ever.*

My bedroom door was open, the typing chair pitched on its side. My floor, which had been full of stuff, was nearly empty. My dresser drawers gaped open. *Mom, are you here? Mom, we've been ransacked! We've been robbed!* I ran down the hall to her bedroom. *Mom, have they hurt you?*

"Are you here?" I called.

Then I felt a jolt of fear. *Was...someone* here?

But by the time I got to her window and looked down into our tiny yard, I had let the truth in. I looked at her empty parking spot and the garbage cans lying empty on their sides—looked at her fluffy-pillowed bed in her un-demolished, untouched room. She'd been here, all right. She'd done what she had done.

I went back down the hallway, stepped over the metal legs of the chair and into Hell. A couple of my posters had been ripped from the wall—Jack White's red guitar torn down the middle, and bits of Narnia still clinging where the thumbtacks held. Aslan stared up at me from a curl of paper on the floor beside a lone, stray sock. My god, had she really thrown out socks and souvenirs and ripped stuff off my walls?

Those two posters—they'd both been gifts from her. I looked into my top dresser drawer. Saw what was missing. Saw what wasn't. I started to grasp the logic of my mother's twisted mind. She'd thrown out all the gifts she'd bought me. Then, momentum growing—like I'd witnessed in her late-night rants—whatever she found on the floor was fair game. The you-can't-even-see-the-floor-in-there-ungrateful-daughter floor. My comforter was rolled back onto the bed like a sad beached whale. Saved because it was only partly on the floor—or too big for her to bother with?

But my backpack. My *backpack*? And the *library* books.

In the lane out back, the garbage cans lying empty on their sides. Today was Tuesday. Garbage day.

It was how many steps to my bed, to look just beneath it to where I'd shoved the prayer book. *Please god may she not have been that thorough.*

But she was.

29 Ruth (*noun:* pity, compassion, sympathy)

It was Mrs. Lynde who found me, kneeling in the lane. Wailing something about a prayer book—that's what she told me later—and clutching a black feather that had been lying beside the garbage cans.

I looked up into her nosy face. *But a kind face?* Through my tears, everything was wavery. At eye level, something gleamed. The bright red fender of her car.

"The *garbage truck*. I need to find it." I think I even grabbed the hem of her coat.

She didn't ask a thing as she drove me through the streets. I glanced over once or twice, in gratitude. Her eyes were on the road, her red beret perched on a cloud of white curls. She just kept driving.

"There it is!" The truck made its way down one of the streets toward the harbor like a big, slow beast. We tailed it. But it was useless. Hopeless. The driver looked at us like we were both crazy. Everything got compacted and mashed up as they went along, he said. He jabbed his thumb toward something he called "the hopper." Plus, they'd already taken a load to the dump.

We went there too—to the dump. And it was equally hopeless. Garbage mixed together. Endless, stinking sea. It was all a blur, like the slow-motion trip from my room to the back lane had been—bits of my life scattered like breadcrumbs through the kitchen and yard.

The drive back to the Hydrostone, though—it had a searing kind of clarity. The streets got more familiar but the eyes I was seeing them with had changed. I rolled down the window and felt the wind hard in my face. I stuck my hand out, still holding the feather. Then I spread my fingers and let it go.

We were on Isleville, nearly at Stairs Place, when we saw it—the tail end of my mother's car zipping into the lane. *Whoa.* "Can you drop me off around the front instead? I need to think for a minute before she sees me."

We rounded the corner and pulled over. I could see the front door of my house halfway down the block. *Home.* But with my clear new eyes I saw it as someplace I wouldn't be staying. Not until my mother, or I, or both of us—*please check all of the above*—got some help.

I needed to say something out loud. There in Mrs. Lynde's front seat, with the air smelling faintly of cinnamon breath mints and Avon perfume, I told the truth (short version though: no juicy details). The truth about my life, and my mother's.

"I don't know how to thank you, Mrs."—I remembered it this time—"O'Dell."

She got something from her glove compartment and pressed it into my hand. I could feel that it was metal, and I thought for a second of a toonie—of how much good a simple toonie had done. But this was a key. A different kind of key—a real one.

"Thank me by taking this. And using it whenever you need to." *No strings attached, no questions asked.* She put it in more or less those words. Somewhere safe for me to go.

It was hard, after the stuff I'd just told her, but I made myself look her in the eye. "I…why would you do this?"

Then we both glanced away. We watched a man walk his dog across the boulevard. "I can still picture the day Tim and Analise brought you home from the hospital. You were just a bundle. It's what neighbors *do* for each other," she said. "Or *should,* at least—try to help. And I've had my suspicions. I should have said something before now."

A few minutes later, I was standing at my own door with my key out. I slipped it into the lock and heard the metallic *thunk* as the tumblers turned over. Like they'd done so many times when things were normal. Or what passed for normal.

She was in the kitchen. It smelled of fresh-brewed coffee, and she was holding her head in both hands.

"It must be hell on a hangover, trashing your daughter's room."

She looked up, eyes bloodshot and with big gray smudges underneath from yesterday's mascara.

"Did you happen to notice something special?" I could hardly breathe. This was the final thread. Last hope. "A really tiny book? An old one?"

She shook her head blankly.

My voice went high. "It was a prayer book?"

She shook her head again. "*What?*"

Oblivious fool. There was nothing more to say. I walked past her. Got two plastic grocery bags from the cupboard. "I'm going upstairs to get my toothbrush and a few things."

When I headed back down she was on the bottom step, as if to block me.

"Jane, we can replace everything that I—"

"*No.* No, we can't." On the hall table beside her sat the jar of quince jelly, still innocently gleaming.

"*Your accent needs some work. But you'll do fine, dear.*"

"You have no idea what damage you've done," I said, and her eyes went to the bags gripped in my hands.

"Where do you think you're going? You've got nowhere to go, Jane. There's just you and me."

"That's not entirely true."

"Of course it is. You can't go imposing on your friends, you know. You'll wear out your welcome."

There was nothing to say, I reminded myself. But I ended up rising to the bait. "It so happens I have a key to someone's house," I told her. "Somewhere I can go when I need to get away. From *you.* And it *isn't* one of my friends."

She gave a weak laugh—part nervous, part mocking. "You're going to move in with some stranger?"

"I'm not *moving in* with anyone. But hardly," I said. "She's known me since I was a baby."

"Oh, *now* I get it." She stepped backward, a bit wobbly, from the stairs down to the floor. "Now I get it." She spat it out this time. "The two-faced bitch."

I just stared at her.

"I kept telling her to stay away from you. But would she leave it alone? 'Analise,' she kept saying, 'I want to be part of Jane's life, but I'll respect your wishes.' Then why'd she keep asking? Wanting to invite you for dinner. Wanting to take you on their stupid vacations—"

What *was* this?

"I should have known she'd go behind my back. Especially since she and Kate moved into town—"

That's when my mouth fell open. *My father's sister. My Aunt Peggy. She'd cared about me all this time?*

My mother's shoulders stiffened and her eyes went wide and then quickly slid away. I was watching it hit her: what I *hadn't* known—and what she'd just told me.

"Jane." She trailed behind me to the door, wringing her hands now—all pathetic. "I was afraid they'd try to keep you, that's all. I thought Peggy and Kate might take you away from me if they found out I had a…that I had a problem."

"Mom." There *was* one more thing to say. "The weird thing is that I *don't* want to leave you. I don't want anyone to take me away from you. *Not even at this minute.* But I'm not going to live like this."

I walked up the hill and sat on the swings where I used to play when I was small. I looked down at the harbor, like Lady Jane and I had done together. Hard to believe it was just this morning.

My two grocery bags of stuff—a few clothes, my makeup, my iPod, and some schoolwork—were on the ground beside me. Pathetic. *Bag girl.* I thought about Peggy, and that took away some of the emptiness. I thought of how I'd always liked her. She'd always been there in my life and then suddenly— when my mother cut off contact—gone.

On my way back down the hill, heading for Mrs. O'Dell's, I remembered a restaurant where Peggy and Kate used to take me, when they lived in the valley. There was a pond nearby where we'd go afterwards, where there were turtles. At first, you'd think they were all hiding. Or just living, I guess, in their underwater world. But then one of us would spot one among the weeds and plankton. And then more would show themselves. You had to stay quiet and look hard to pick out the intricate patterns on their shells. You had to look carefully to catch them breaking through the surface.

She's living in one of the houses we looked at from the hill. A girl with pale skin and freckles. She brushes back a strand of hair. Cut short now. Dyed magenta. There are clues all around the room, if you know what to look for. The poster of a rolling green field, with hedgerows. The vintage jacket draped over her chair. Velvet. Creamy lace at the sleeves. The small gold cross around her neck. Not just an ornament. Her phone rings and the ringtone makes me want to cheer. Lute music! Even better is how her face lights up. "Do you want to hang out?" *she says into the phone, using the words I taught her. Then she pulls on her jacket and heads down the stairs, putting her earbuds in, smiling.*

Where am I? I thought as I woke up. An unfamiliar dark green on the walls around me. Mrs. O'Dell's. Light sifted in through the curtains, and I closed my eyes, not wanting to let in what that meant. It meant a new day here; time had moved two days in Jane's world.

"My only prayer is that he dispatch me quickly."

My friend, my lady—she was gone.

30 Fleet-winged (*adjective*: swift of flight)

Lady Jane Dudley—better known by her birth name Jane
Grey—was beheaded on Tower Green, Tower of London, on
the 12th day of February, 1554. In keeping with the custom,
she had to stand and wait a full five minutes in case the queen
sent a reprieve. But no one came to save her.

She walked to the scaffold on the arm of Sir John Bridges,
Lieutenant of the Tower. She carried a tiny leather-bound
book, the Booke of Prayre. Her closest servants, Mistress
Ellen and Mistress Tilney, walked behind her, crying so hard
that they had to hold each other up.

Witnesses wrote down what Jane said: "Good people,
I come hither to die...The fact, indeed, against the queen's
highness was unlawful, and the consenting thereunto by me."
She also said she'd had no "desire" for the crown and had
done nothing to "procure" it. "I do wash my hands thereof in
innocency." She didn't plead. But she didn't back down.

The Catholic priest who was there at Jane's side fell
apart, and witnesses said Jane held his hand to comfort him.
Then she asked him to join her in the reading of her favorite
psalm:

Have mercy upon me O God,
according to thy loving-kindness:
according unto the multitude of thy
tender mercies, blot out my transgressions...

I closed my project and stuffed it back into the book bag Mrs. O'Dell had lent me, with my other papers and things. It was all I had left, but I didn't feel like ever looking at it again.

I got up and started pacing around the room. At the window, I lifted one of the slats in Ms. MacAllistair's venetian blind. Tom, Megan, and Crisco were standing there. I looked at the clock—3:41—and remembered I was supposed to be meeting them. Peeking down at the three of them, I willed myself to come back, bit by bit, to my own life. The one I could do something with; the one I was beginning to sort out.

Megan shifted from one foot to the other with a dramatic shiver, sending ripples the length of her hair. Crisco, with both hands buried deep in her pockets, looked like she was humming to herself. One thing I was starting to like, I realized, was how she'd seem to be off in her own world, then she'd make some comment that was totally right on. Maybe Crisco talked so loud because she was speaking across some kind of divide. Maybe we were all a bit more unusual than we looked.

But I wouldn't be introducing them to someone who was *a lot* more unusual. No "Matilda." No new friend.

Tom took out his cell, and in a second mine began to ring. I didn't answer. I watched him try another number. Home? Was she there? Would she pick up?

He slipped the phone back into his pocket and looked up, like he was scanning for faces. I stepped further to one side. Part of me was way beyond embarrassment—had been ever since Mrs. O'Dell found me kneeling in the lane. But I didn't want them to see me. Not right now, looking down at life—at our lives—from the other side of this window. Tom had a CD review to write tonight and Crisco had an art class. Megan and I were supposed to study together while I babysat. But here I was, like YOU ARE HERE, waiting for Ms. MacAllistair to get off the phone. She was down the hall, pulling together some contact information that I'd asked her for: an Alateen group, a counselor I could talk to, some counselors' names for my mother—if she was willing to go.

It wasn't fair. But I was the lucky one, I knew that. I had people I could turn to. And choices that did seem like real possibilities. Not like Lady Jane.

My possibilities could work, I figured, if I added them together. The names I'd be getting right now would help. And I'd have Mrs. O'Dell's place to go to. It was a bit close for comfort—I'd felt very aware of that last night—but it would do in emergencies. And Megan's place. And Traci's too. I knew I could stay with either of them sometimes, now that I had nothing to hide. And then there was the phone number I'd found last night—my aunt's number. I was feeling less shaky now. Ready to talk to her. I'd call as soon as I figured she was home from work.

"Hey, Megan," I whispered through the glass, "you've been right all along. There's so much I haven't told you." I'd call *her* later too. And Tom, of course. And I'd call Crisco too.

I watched the three of them walk away, Tom casting one last glance over his shoulder. I was just about to let the blind flick shut when a crow stepped into sight, picking its way across the half-frozen ground. You might think I imagined this, but it seemed too big. Like, several sizes.

Odin? I pulled the slats open wider to get a better look.

To make it all this way on your damaged wings.

Author's Note

The historical events in this book really happened.

A few of the things Lady Jane Grey says were her actual words. For instance, the names she calls the other Jane during their argument come from her letter to a Protestant friend who had converted to Catholicism; and "How long wilt thou be absent... Is thy mercy clean gone?" is from a prayer she wrote.

Her *Booke of Prayre* exists (or at least one that is generally accepted as hers), and it contains her handwritten message to Lieutenant Bridges. Jane carried the book and read Psalm 51 aloud before her execution. The book is owned by the British Library, where I saw it on display. You can view it online by searching for "Lady Jane Grey's prayer book" under Contents at:

www.bl.uk/catalogues/illuminatedmanuscripts/search2.asp

Lady Jane did resist marrying Guildford Dudley, and her parents did treat her the way I've described. There's been much speculation about her feelings for Edward Seymour. But it's never been proved that she was in love with him; the letter in this novel is my own invention. So are two books that I quote from in the novel—Jane's English textbook and *Lady Jane Grey, a 16th-Century Tragedy*.

I've also taken three other liberties: I've modified the language by replacing "thou" with "you" in most cases (the usage
varied at the time, depending on context); and I've described
London's streetscape as it was in Jane's approximate, rather than
exact, time (some sources were from up to fifty years later).
On a less historical note: there is a Citadel High in Halifax,
but I've invented most of the details about it.

My research took me to dozens of print and online materials, including biographies, historical texts, primary sources,
and historical fiction. Among the most useful or notable were
Lady Jane Grey by Hester W. Chapman, *The Nine Days Queen*
by Karleen Bradford, *The Frozen Thames* by Helen Humphreys,
Shakespeare's Words: A Glossary and Language Companion com-
piled by David Crystal and Ben Crystal, and *Survivors: Children
of the Halifax Explosion* by Janet F. Kitz.

Acknowledgements

This book owes some of its best moves to Ann Featherstone, my astute and talented editor at Pajama Press; and to Tim Wynne-Jones, who mentored me when I was writing an early draft. Extra thanks to Ann for keeping her cool and helping me keep mine. And thanks to everyone at the press—especially Gail Winskill for her enthusiasm.

The book probably owes its life to the Nova Scotia Department of Tourism, Culture and Heritage, Culture Division. Their generous funding gave me what I needed most: time to write, and a research trip to London. Thanks also to the Humber School for Writers for the mentorship program with Tim and a Writers' Trust scholarship.

I'm grateful to Cynthia Gatto of Halifax Public Libraries, for letting me adjust my work schedule during my year at Alderney Gate; and to many friends and colleagues for their suggestions. Julie Vandervoort and Sandra Barry gave me feedback early on, as did Norene Smiley and everyone in her workshop at the Fed (Writers' Federation of Nova Scotia). Much later, Mary Bruno provided helpful insight into "pretending."

Jill MacLean and my daughter Jeanna Greene deserve special thanks for critiquing an earlier version—and more: a huge thanks to Jill for the introduction to Pajama Press; and to Jeanna for reading the whole manuscript again at the eleventh hour and making great catches and suggestions.

Finally, here's to some of the encouraging and patient people in my life: the previously mentioned Jill and Jeanna, and Jeanna's boyfriend, Scott MacMillan; the Amys (Zierler and Whitmore); Charlotte Lindgren; Dilys Leman; donalee ("you're a good woman") Moulton; James Suffidy; Jean Single (for countless talks); Judy Miller (for the duration); Maureen Hynes; and Wynne Jordan.